A Gang

By: EL Griffin

Drew

"Wake the fuck up!"

I heard Saint's voice in the distance. I forced my eyes open, blinking repeatedly until my vision cleared. Lifting my head off the steering wheel, I was hit with an instant throbbing pain. I reached up trying to feel the damage from the impact. The amount of blood on my hand let me know my shit was split open. I probably had a concussion.

No moon or stars were out tonight, leaving nothing but darkness in front of me. But from behind, those same bright ass headlights shined in the car lighting up the interior. The lights started moving.

I gathered my thoughts quick as hell and turned around. The mothafuckas were backing up trying to leave the scene. That's where Saint must have yelled out from. I needed to stop them.

I hopped out with my strap ready, pointed in the direction of the other car. Aiming the gun, I squeezed the trigger unloading the full clip. Not a single gotdamn bullet made contact. I never missed my target bad like this. Damn, my eye sight was fucked up.

I rubbed the side of my forehead that wasn't leaking, trying to clear my vision again. Then shook it back and forth until I could see half way decent. The vehicle sped off, along with my opportunity to stop the mothafuckas inside of it.

We were in the city but the hospital sat back secluded from other buildings. It was off the main highway and had a long ass drive up to it. In the matter of a couple minutes shit had gone from bad to fucking worse. Now it was just a matter of time before 12 rode up on us.

I threw my pistol far off into the ditch. Hopefully, the police wouldn't look for something they didn't know was there. Then I could come back and get the shit later. Saint dropped his tool back in the warehouse for the team to pick up. But I still had mine on me. My misstep could link me to bodies and cause me to catch a murder wrap. But I couldn't be worried about that shit right now.

I jumped back in my car fast as hell, putting it in drive and pulling up the rest of the way to the emergency entrance. Driving with flat tires and no fucking traction. The rims grating against the pavement, making a sharp ass squealing sound.

Fuck my injuries and the gun I just threw. I couldn't even worry about Saint right

6

now. *My priority was making sure Nya was straight. Then I could worry about where the fuck Saint was and who the mothafuckas were that took him.*

I opened the driver side door, stepping out. Then moved to the back to pull Nya out as steady as possible. There was no telling what had her knocked out, but her ass was still out of it even after all the shit went down. The same way she was when Saint first picked her up off the desk.

The sirens in the distance were getting closer. I needed to hurry the fuck up.

"HELP!!!" I shouted loud as hell.

Some fat ass man walked out of the automatic doors. His looked changed real quick when he saw Nya laying limp in my arms. He turned back around and yelled inside for more help. Then rushed over to Nya followed by two other nurses hurrying through the front entrance.

"This is NyAsia Miller. She's pregnant." I handed her over to their care, laying her down on the hospital gurney.

I wanted to put some distance between her and the police when they pulled up. I didn't want none of this to come back on her if I could help it. That was part of the responsibility of being in the game. To keep the people you cared about safe. Saint would expect nothing less from me. The same way I *would want him to look out for my woman, even if she wasn't his sister.*

Damn, Jolie was gonna be fucked up behind all this. I turned around and started walking away, back down the small hill. Making my way over to the crash scene where only my car was left. One of the nurse's yelled after me trying to get more information. But I kept right on walking ignoring her.

I pulled out my phone and sent Jolie a quick text in code letting her know to come out here to the hospital.

"Nya's sick."

After it was sent, I turned my phone off and threw the shit in some bushes. Seconds later, an unmarked explorer and a cop car like the one that caused this shit turned the corner. I put my hands in the air ready for the mothafuckas.

Six months later...

Nya

"Where are you? I can't do this without you."

I woke myself with the same words I repeated each time I had this damn dream. The same shit that haunted my sleep for the past six months. But of course it came to an end. The familiar ending I dreaded.

It was always the same. I was pregnant mirroring real life, growing each time it reoccurred. Everything was vivid as hell and realistic. It was like Saint was really here with me. From the smell of his cologne down to the feel of his solid body on mine.

We were laid up in bed, him holding me with me tracing the outline of his tattoo of my initials on his chest. The same way he always loved form me to do, with my hands on his body connected to him. Then out of nowhere he would start to fade away. Like a damn ghost in a movie.

I would try and hold Saint's body tighter to stop him from disappearing on me, only to be met with nothing. In the blink of an eye he would be gone again and I would be left crying in my dream, just to wake up to wet cheeks and asking the same damn question over and over again... "Where was he?"

With the back of my hand, I wiped away the wetness on my face and sat up in bed. I might as well get this day started, even though it was only 4:30 in the morning.

I had enough school work to keep my ass busy. So I reached down to grab my work, holding my huge stomach with my other hand. My due date was in 2 weeks and for the most part I was ready. I looked forward to finally being able to hold my son in my arms. But it was bittersweet.

This pregnancy had been anything but easy. From before Saint was gone even. I was sick all the damn time and had weird ass cravings. My son meant the world to me, but a bitch was ready to NOT be pregnant anymore.

Then Saint was taken and my fucking heart along with him. I really went through it. I still was.

I put a mental wall back up to get through and endure his absence. I needed to be strong for our child. Just like before, when I experienced hell at my aunt's and I did what I needed to do for Terrell. Some shit was more important than your feelings. And for my son I would do anything.

When I woke up in the hospital and found out Saint was nowhere to be found, I nearly lost my mind. I went crazy trying to get up out of there, demanding answers. Drew explained everything, but nothing made sense. I cried for hours and didn't want to talk to anyone. I didn't even want to see Terrell when he tried to come in.

Later that same day when the doctor's told me that my baby's health was in jeopardy my energy shifted. I forced myself to get my shit together despite my heart being broken.

That nigga that took me used chloroform on me to knock my ass out. He used it once in the car and then another time after I woke up inside the warehouse. That shit made my pregnancy high risk and the doctor's kept me on bed rest for two more months to check the baby's growth. According to them there might still be some possible side effects, like low birth weight or an underdeveloped nervous system.

But from how this boy moved and the bond I already felt with him, I wasn't doubting his strength at all. I had to keep faith in my son and in Saint coming back to us. I was waiting for the day where Saint would be reunited with us. That's how I faced each day; optimistic and waiting for my nigga to come back to me.

In the meantime, my classes were the only thing keeping my mind off the reality that Saint might not be coming home soon or ever. I refused to believe that shit though, just like I didn't give up hope when he was in a coma even with the odds stacked against him.

My focus and drive were paying off at least. I was doing my damn thing when it came to school. It was my refuge right now and I threw myself into the work a hundred percent. My classes were back to back Monday through Thursday. I was taking more classes than my advisor wanted me to with 28 credits. On the weekends I spent all my extra time hitting the books.

I knew once the baby was born, I would have to slow down some. But after a short break, my ass was getting right back to it. I went 10 long years struggling not thinking I would ever have a chance to even finish high school. I wasn't letting go of my dreams for anything. All I knew was hustle so being a bomb ass mother was another role I would play. It wasn't stopping shit.

Terrell was doing great in school right along with me. After the chaos of last year, he completed the necessary homeschool and maintained a 4.0 GPA. I gave him a choice of doing homeschool again or going back for his

Senior year. He wanted to be back in school with the friends he made out here and I didn't blame him. He deserved to have some damn security and I was determined to give him and my son that shit, if it killed me.

I pulled the laptop out of my backpack. Ready to get to work and keep my mind off the dream that woke me up in the first place. I only had a few more days before I took an early finish for my courses, a week before the rest of the school let out for Christmas break.

Today was Saturday so my plans consisted of homework and lounging around the house. Later I was going over to Jolie's to catch up and spend time with her and my niece. Jolie stepped up, becoming a mother to two kids and kept going without missing a beat. All by her damn self. I hoped I could have the parenting shit down like she did.

A few hours into busting out my paper, a message came through on one of my cell phones. That was another thing. Since Saint wasn't here right now, me and Jolie were temporarily running his organization in New Orleans. We really didn't have a choice since Saint set it up that way in case he wasn't able to.

With Drew's backing nobody questioned the shit for the most part. All we had to do was schedule shipments and drop-offs of the product and cash. We stayed behind the scenes only dealing with a few niggas that ran the traps. Every Monday and Friday we met up at the house downtown and went over the books after we got the cash.

The message came from my work phone. It was from Jolie and all she sent was some simple shit,

"DWNTWN 9:00".

That shit was bizarre as hell. Something was up. We didn't meet up at new times unless there was. We followed the same precautions Saint took and didn't discuss business over phones. All I could do was wait a couple more hours and see what the shit meant.

The thought of it having something to do with Saint crossed my mind, but that was just wishful thinking. I stared at the words on the computer screen in front of me and pushed those thoughts away, getting back to the essay instead.

Saint

4:30 in the morning wasn't shit to me, neither was waking up feeling the cold steel beneath the thread bare mattress I slept on. A street nigga built for this life could handle prison. But being away from my family, not knowing what the fuck happened the night I was put in this bitch was what was fucking with me.

That night we handled the niggas that took Nya, just to end up having Pedro's bitch ass finally show his face. He picked the worst time to decide to grow some balls.

Next time I saw his ass I was killing the mothafucka. No matter what it meant for me. He was always hiding behind shit. Even now his ass sent me off to this Mexican pen, El Hungo, to play fucking games instead of just taking me out like he should have done. He wanted me dead so bad but wasted all this fucking time leaving me alive.

It didn't take long to figure out what his ass was up to after I got here. He wanted to make me fear him, but he didn't understand a nigga like me didn't fear a mothafucka alive. Not that I was cocky, everybody was dying one day and if today was my day so be it. Fuck living scared behind the shit.

15

He thought shit was gonna be simple because I was alone, outnumbered on his turf. But things didn't go the way he thought, just like all his pussy ass plans. I got my ass whooped the first day when five mothafuckas jumped me. I put up a fucking fight though and laid a few of his cartel members out in the process. But the next day was a different story.

Pedro always underestimated me. He tried to look down on me and thought of me as just another nigga that was replaceable. He might have been a cartel boss, but it turned out his organization wasn't any competition down here compared to my supplier. My new plug wasn't a cartel boss himself, but he was high up in an opposing cartel that was a whole lot fucking bigger and more ruthless than Pedro's.

On that second day when some of the same mothafuckas with Pedro's team made their move out on the yard shit changed. About 20 other mothafuckas I hadn't even talked to came and stood between me and Pedro's bitch ass team, letting the whole prison know that I was under their protection. Even in Mexico penitentiary rules were the same. So Pedro took another fucking L and I was serving him another one when I got the fuck out of here.

I wasn't bitch made no matter what and even with their backing, I stayed fucking ready. There wasn't room for weakness or stupidity behind these walls. I wasn't outnumbered any more but alliances could shift when it came to power. Mothafuckas always wanted more of that shit. Inside was just another version of the same street shit that I had been living since I was a kid.

Pedro couldn't do shit about the pull I had in here either. The opposing cartel was the same one he went up against in Houston. He got the upper hand with the hit I did in their blood feud, but I picked the right fucking side in the end.

Every time I thought about this shit it was like a big fucking joke. All this over his hoe ass daughter. Martina was dead along with her pops as soon as I was free.

The charges Pedro got me sent here for were some trafficking shit with planting dope on me and using his connects with the Mexican Police after driving me across the border that night.

Even in a hard ass prison like El Hungo this shit was nothing but time. I could do my time without a second thought but that was before shawty came back in my life and I had a baby on the way. A bitch could really fuck up your head.

I sat up, then placed my feet on the floor. I slept with the old ass sandals on me feet, not taking them off in this bitch period. Standing in front of my metal bunk, still adjusting my eyes to the bright ass lights.

They kept the lights on 24 hours a day here to try and keep riots and killings down. But it really wasn't stopping shit. The cartels ran this place for the most part. The first few weeks I had a headache all day every day but your body adjusts to conditions in prison after a while.

This place was unlike any prison back in the US. All your rights and shit were nonexistent here. It was set up in the middle of a damn desert which meant it was hot as hell during the day and cold as fuck at night. I was ready to get the fuck out of Mexico for good, after six months.

I put my grey sweatshirt on and walked over to the front of the cell. They used a fingerprint and picture ID system to do roll call three times a day after each meal. With all these precautions you would think that it was hard as hell for mothafuckas to break out. But if El Chapo could do it, so the fuck could I.

Nobody back home knew I was here and I hadn't directly talked to my new connect or any of the higher ups with the cartel I was protected by. That was supposed to change soon. One of the inmates was my contact. He was giving me messages from "el jefe". According to him there was a plan in the works to get me the fuck out of here.

I assumed these mothafuckas were doing all this for a reason. It had to be a business move on their part. I didn't even speak Spanish but some of the basic shit, so I didn't understand everything I was told. But for them to go to these lengths protecting me it had to be about the fucking bread. I was a business man myself so that shit was the only thing that made sense.

After putting my finger on the small pad, I followed the line walking out of the open cell door past the two guards standing on either side. We headed down two levels going through another set of cage doors opening to let us pass.

We walked like well-trained soldiers down to the food hall at 4:30 in the fucking morning like it was normal. It was too early for bullshit so it was usually the quietest time of the day in here. Inside the food hall there were small tables and plastic chairs set up where three people could sit to a table at a time. Meal times were staggered so all the inmates weren't in this bitch at the same time.

It was the same Mexican food I had been eating for months now and hated.

Peppers, rice and chicken early in the damn morning. It wasn't the good shit either. Just like American prisons with the bland ass flavor and nasty ass food. But it what was it was for the time being.

Javier came over a few minutes later and sat down. He didn't waste any time getting right to the shit that was on his mind. Before another one of the gang members sat down at our table, he said some shit that caught me off guard.

"Tu hermano esta en Mexico meeting with el jefe."

That was all he got out before the other member sat down, silencing him. It was short and didn't tell me much, but the mix of English with Spanish was enough for me to understand the meaning. Things were starting to happen now. My mother's family had pull worldwide. If Juan knew I was here and really was about all that family shit he was spitting now would be the time to prove it. I still didn't trust his ass though, so I would just have to wait and see.

I continued to keep my head down and eat the fucking food on my tray like it was the best thing I had eaten in months. Shit, even with the questionable news about Juan, it tasted like it was.

Jolie

Waking up at the crack of dawn was nothing new to me. Having a four year old and a newborn laying up under me, kept me up many nights. First thing when the light shone through the windows, both of them were ready to wake my ass up.

This morning was no different. BJ tugged at the covers standing by the side of the bed trying to wake me up. He was finally sleeping in his own bed. With Terrell and Nya living at Saint's it gave me enough room to set up a room for him along with a new nursery for Joy. That was what I named our daughter.

She was the joy I thought I would never find again. The moment I held her in my arms I was complete. Despite losing Buck and being a hot mess for most of my pregnancy she changed my life. Little by little I was piecing it back together. Having both Joy and her big brother with me in this house finally made it home.

I always loved children which is why I was a teacher. But I was scared to death of not doing shit the right way, having stability and all the things a person was supposed to have before starting a family. I thought it would fuck something up like how my childhood was fucked up.

It turned out my life had a mind of its own and everything was working out the exact opposite way I planned for. It was funny how sometimes the things you think are gonna break you or make life worse, actually wind up bringing the most happiness. Every time I looked my daughter in the eyes, I was at peace.

I still missed Buck and ended up crying myself to sleep sometimes. I thought about the love and life we would never get to build. But now I knew that I could go on without him. I couldn't let our children experience pain because he would never want that for them. He loved BJ despite having a hard ass time showing love to anyone.

That was why it was easy for me to take care of Buck's son as if he was my own. It wasn't a burden to me, but a blessing to get to have both our kids grow up together in the same home. I damn sure hadn't heard a peep from his real mother.

I played sleep for a few more tugs on the cover from BJ.

"Ma J, Ma J." his cute little voice said, sounding impatient.

I lunged forward grabbing ahold of his little body and catching him off guard. Wrapping my arms around him, pulling him in for a hug squeezing tight. He laughed and tried to back away from the kisses I laid on his chubby cheeks.

I finally let go, grinning at him. He lifted his hand and tried to wipe away the invisible kiss marks from his face.

"ahhh, mane."

I swear this little boy was too much already. He was still a little boy, only four years old trying to be all big and tough like a man not wanting me to kiss him.

I sat up in bed and rubbed my hand across the top of his head. I was letting his hair grow longer, and it was almost ready to get locked up. I always tried to get Buck to let his hair grow out and lock it up. But his ass wouldn't do it.

Finally, I got him to agree to at least let BJ do it once his hair grew more. Buck would have looked good with them and now his little twin would be rocking them. Of course Buck only agreed after I put the pussy on his ass. So now I was seeing the promise through. It was just another way to keep his memory alive. It was a story I could tell BJ about when he was a little older, leaving out the sex part of course.

"Alright, but you know you're so cute baby I couldn't help it. I know you're getting big now. Do you think we should wake up Joy?" I asked, knowing he was gonna be all about it.

23

He jumped up and down and ran up to the bed all excited. I reminded him to do it gently. He got all serious and set his mouth in a plastered on straight line. It was so funny how serious he took his big brother role already. I knew Joy was gonna pay for it later when it came to the niggas she wanted to kick it with. But I didn't want it any other way.

Joy was only 3 months old, but already showing her personally. She was a happy baby, but the moment she didn't get her way she showed out. It was partially my fault though. I wasn't one of those mothers that let her baby cry. If she wanted something I tried to give it to her and now hardly anybody could hold her rotten ass.

BJ crawled slowly to the middle of the bed atop the down comforter and placed a single kiss on top of Joy's small forehead. Me and buck had did the damn thing with our daughter. She was beautiful, with a full head of thick curls and dimples in her cheeks like mine. She took after me with her light complexion but her eyes matched BJ's, taking after her daddy.

"Joy, wake up." It only took him one time and her eyes popped open.

A lot of new mothers might not want their baby to wake up, but Joy was already on a basic sleep schedule at night and she always listened to her big brother when he tried to wake her up. Let me do the same shit and she would end up crying after I woke her up. Their bond was solid already. Just like how Saint was always my protector and the person I looked up to. I wanted that for my daughter.

Thinking about Saint, got me caught up in my feelings for a minute. I missed the hell out of my brother and thought about him constantly. Since the night he was taken and called me to tell me to take precautions, I hadn't heard his voice one time. I still kept faith that he was alive and until we got word otherwise that was how we were keeping it.

I reached for my phone and pulled it off the charger seeing some missed calls. 2 from Drew and the others from one of our lieutenants that ran the traps out here. I ignored the few texts I saw from Drew and went to take care of business first.

I hit the send button calling Boy's number back, wondering what caused him to call so early in the morning. It was almost 7, but the streets never slept so there was no telling what was up. Boy was the next in charge behind us out here. It was still hard to believe that me and Nya were really running this operation while Saint was gone. But we stepped up and did what we had to do in his absence. We couldn't let what happened last time happen again. Saint learned from the past, and that was why he continued to thrive when others crashed and burned in this life.

"What's up?" I got right to it when I heard his phone pick up.

"We need to meet."

"9 o'clock." I kept it to a minimum.

It was clear that whatever he had to talk about was serious enough not to mention anything over the phone. That let me know it probably wasn't anything good. In the 6 months of handling shit, we hadn't run into any major problems. But when I went on a brief break from having Joy, Nya did have to deal with some small time shit with a couple of the corner boys.

She was a real gangsta at heart just like my brother. The more work she put in, the more confidence she had about the shit too. I just hoped that when my brother came back she was able to give it up. I knew for a fact he wouldn't want either of us involved in anything more than we had to be. But that was gonna be when he came back. For now, we had to do what we had to do. When she told me how she handled the shit I was even more convinced she was the perfect match for Saint. She was off in the head just like his crazy ass. My girl was a stone cold mothafucka.

She was also smart as hell and finally getting to pursue her dreams, which is why all calls came my way first, in case she was in class. It was how we wanted to chain of command to flow. But seeing as it was serious I went ahead and sent her a message.

Now, I could give my attention to the other messages from Drew. A smile came to my face as I read the two simple texts, and butterflies formed in the pit of my stomach. Drew was becoming more and more special to me.

After the night where he ended up saving Nya and Saint was taken, I switched up shit on him. I realized more than ever that I did have real feelings for him. All that came to the surface when I thought something might have happened to him. It wasn't love, yet. But over the past year my feelings only grew stronger.

So far we hadn't had sex. I wasn't ready for all that yet, so I didn't go along when he wanted to define us as a committed relationship. I wasn't dumb for a man in the least. I knew if I wasn't giving him any pussy he would be getting it from someone else. I would never be number 2 to another bitch period. So until I was ready to feel the dick, we were just "dating". I had thought about what it would be like to feel him inside me more and more lately.

We had gotten pretty close last time he was in town and we spent the weekend together. But I stopped the shit right before he had my panties off. I couldn't even let him eat my pussy because I knew that his dick would follow. I wasn't one of those bitches that was satisfied with just a tease. When I went with it, I went all the way out there.

I texted him back and added an emoji kiss, all that corny shit. He was a gangsta, but he loved when I showed feelings for him. I knew his ass was new to all this like I was. All our past relationships were tainted in some way. As much and as long as I loved Buck, we were never out in the open with it until the very end, when it was too late. Being taken on dates and romanced was new to me. And all Drew's ex bitches, were the most ratchet gold digging hoes you could think of. He didn't really give a fuck about any of them to treat like an actual girlfriend. What we were doing now was some real grown shit.

He was coming in town tonight and invited me to dinner. I agreed even after how far things went last time. A part of me knew that tonight would be different than all the other nights we shared. I wanted to let him in all the way.

Nya loved to watch the kids and always begged me to drop them off more, so I knew she would be cool with keeping them for me tonight. I was so happy to have my best friend back. It's amazing how forgiveness can help you get past the worst days of your life.

Since it was Saturday, all I had to do was head to this meeting and then hang with the babies until later. I called the babysitter to have her come over this morning around 8:30, to give me enough time to make it downtown in the traffic.

It was time to get this day going and make the most of it. That was the same thought I tried to have every morning. I wanted to live day by day and make the most of it. Because one thing I clung to after losing Buck and not knowing where my brother was, was that you never knew what the day will hold or when it will be your last day with your loved ones. It was tragic but true.

Nya

I headed downtown earlier than the meeting was scheduled for. After I got the message from Jolie, I couldn't get any more school work done. All my thoughts kept going back to Saint. I couldn't seem to get him off my mind today. Some days were worse than others. The panic and anxiety of not knowing what the future held was almost too much to bare sometimes.

I pulled up to the house and parked across the street. Every time I came here I felt Saint's presence in everything. When I made it to the door, I unlocked it then disabled the security system. Turning on the lights before taking my time walking around the small house.

There wasn't much we kept in the place, except a few bottles of water and some canned food in case of emergency. In the master bedroom there was also two safes. One was full of clean money that couldn't be traced and the other held a few guns and passports, with fake ID's for the three of us and Terrell. The babies didn't need one yet, but soon enough they would be included. Saint hid the safes below floor boards in the closet. It was some new shit that he added since getting gunned down.

Knowing that I was in the game, standing tall and handling shit for my nigga while he wasn't able to give me a sense of pride. I never knew that I would actually enjoy being a part of all this though. I couldn't even lie this lifestyle gave me a rush and let me get out some of the aggression I had pent up inside when necessary. Like when I handled those two niggas a few months ago.

I took a seat at the dining room table. The table was where we always conducted business. I didn't want the lieutenants thinking we were soft or couldn't handle ourselves. It was no secret that insecure men hated letting women run shit. That's why me and sis had to stay on top of everything. So far we had kept shit running smooth and there wasn't any major problems.

Right before 9:00, Jolie came in the door after using her key to unlock it like I did. She was smiling and looking beautiful as ever. She had this new glow to her since having the baby. If I didn't know better, I would think Jolie had a nigga in her life. There was something more uplifting than I had seen in her in a long ass time.

"Hey sis." I called out.

"What's up girl? I'm glad you're here before Boy arrives so we can figure out the move. After he tells us what's up, I'm gonna

31

let you lead. You got the head for this shit, I'm just more of the business mind in it. Whatever you feel is best, I'm with the shit. Okay?"

I nodded my head in agreement. "Makes sense, but if you got some feelings on it, don't hesitate to be real with me after he's gone. I want real ass opinions to back me up." I added.

Being in charge was some big shoes to fill. Jolie was right, we couldn't hesitate the slightest bit when it came to responding. That would show weakness. Where a nigga, especially one like Saint could discuss shit, me and Jolie didn't have any leeway. We would get eaten alive in these streets otherwise. And all this shit was eat or be eaten, kill or be killed.

"You got it. So how's Kwamir doing?" She asked. Knowing I was getting impatient with this pregnancy shit. I had decided to go with the name Kwamir, named after his father.

"Girl, he's a mess already. Kicking me all damn night. This little boy just needs to stop being stubborn and make his debut already."

I rubbed my stomach. I loved my son with everything, but I damn sure was done with being pregnant at this point. It was time he come on out.

"He's gotta do shit his way, just like his daddy. You know how that goes." She let out a laugh. She was speaking nothing but facts. He was his father's son already.

"I see you're smiling looking all happy early in the morning! I should be asking you questions... What you got goin' on?"

My interest piqued since I first saw her walk in the door with that extra bounce in her step. I knew my best friend. Her light bright ass blushed, cheeks turning pink then looked down for a second. Yup some shit was up with my girl for sure.

"What makes you think I got something going on? Can't a bitch just be happy? I mean I got two beautiful babies at home, and it's a beautiful day. I'm sitting here with my beautiful pregnant best friend!" She said being even more extra, I couldn't help but laugh. This bitch was really feeling some type of way.

"So what about the nigga in your life? Is he beautiful too?" I had to ask.

She started laughing right along with my ass from the question.

"Well... since you asked, YES bitch he is BEAUTFIFUL". That was all she got out before there was a knock at the front door, ending the conversation abruptly. But I was gonna follow up on this shit. Jolie must really be feeling some type of way about this

33

mystery man. It had to be more serious if she was actually admitting to some shit.

Jolie was so in love with Buck. Real ass love. After he died I didn't know if my girl was ever gonna be happy again. I didn't judge her for moving on. She was young, smart and deserved to find some happiness of her own. Buck would want that shit for her anyway. It wasn't fair for her to be miserable for the rest of her life.

I stood up to get the door, but Jolie waved me off. She always looked out for me like this since she dropped the baby and my ass was still waddling around. A couple months ago we both were a sight to see. Pregnant and telling these street niggas what to do. At first they tried not to take us serious, but when I put the operation on halt for a week, they all got in line real fucking quick. Nobody wanted their pockets empty. The rest was history. Pregnant or not we some hustlers at heart.

Boy came in looking like he was just coming in off the block. He sat down in a chair opposite of me on the other end of the table. His name suggested he was young, but he was actually the same age as Saint. He did have a baby face. The bitches loved that shit, but he was solid with his baby mama. She was cool as hell too. I met her a few times and she was real low key and a rida for sure.

He was the highest lieutenant we had, and Saint definitely chose the right man.

"What's going on?" I asked.

"We got a problem. Those downtown niggas cut prices, and shit's affecting our bread. It really hit hard over the last week. I was waiting for confirmation before bringing it to ya'll. Then last night we caught up with one of the niggas on our team that hadn't shown his face on the Bank in over a week. I was hearing some questionable shit about his ass. It turned out he thought he could just switch sides. He said, wasn't no money over here anymore, and he wasn't working for some bitches... No offense. This shit could snowball fast as fuck, mane."

I leaned into the table resting my elbow on it then bringing my hand to the side of my face out of habit, thinking about the best way to cut this shit off and stop the bleeding. What would Saint do?

I always tried to think of what he would do and make him proud. He stayed more than a step ahead at all times. He was the one who formed the Choppa City Cartel to begin with. That was it! I knew what we needed to do.

"Bring his ass to the spot and handle him. Keep prices the same until I say otherwise. These niggas want some problems, that's what they fuck they're gonna get. No

35

other moves for now against anyone from that side. Round up a few loyal niggas you trust and have them on standby. Don't tell them shit, we need to keep this quiet."

Like a solid ass soldier he didn't ask any more questions, even though I saw the wheels turning in his head trying to piece together what I was up to. But it wasn't for him to know. It was a mistake to speak on shit unless necessary. When the time came he would have his role to play. I appreciated his loyalty to Saint and our team for bringing this to me and Jolie and not switching up like this other nigga did.

"Bet. We're good over here." He reassured. I didn't doubt he would keep his word.

"This shit is temporary, Boy. Saint is your boss. We're just running shit 'til he touches back down, know that."

"You aint gotta tell me shit shawty. Saint came to me about this shit before ya'll even stepped up."

Damn that was news to me. No wonder he never questioned where Saint was and he vouched for us to the rest of the team. It made sense now. Saint had really learned from how shit went down before. He never ceased to amaze me. He was the fucking truth and for that, his organization was still gonna be running at the top just like he left the bitch.

I nodded my head as Boy got up leaving the house. It was time that I put in a call and take care of business. No more playing around.

Saint

I laid in my bunk head covered, attempting to block out the constant light to get some damn sleep. But all my mind kept going to was NyAsia and how she was doing. Hopefully Juan was really down here making shit happen. Since being backed by the CJNG who was teamed up with the Sinaloa cartel, I wasn't worried about shit Pedro's bitch ass could do to me. Matter of fact, his ass should be worried about me now.

Him and his hoe ass daughter were as good as dead when I busted out of this bitch. I was coming after everyone that fucked with my family, on God. I wasn't playing with any of these mothafuckas anymore. I realized that even though I thought I was being smart and waiting to take care of shit, that there couldn't be no more hesitation. I was murdering them all. That meant I was looking for those other bitches too. I didn't forget about the loose ends we left that night.

As far as Nya went I had to keep hope alive that she was straight. That Drew handled things, woke up and made sure she got to the fucking hospital. We were right up the road when the fake ass mothafuckas shot out our tires. I had to keep believing her and my seed were good. Otherwise what the fuck was any of this for?

I heard the cell gate sliding open. That shit caught my attention since it was the middle of the damn night and everybody in this bitch was asleep. Voices from the men in my cell block started escalating into a full blown argument out of nowhere.

I lifted the cover from my face and looked at the scene unfolding. I didn't have a fucking clue what they were shouting at each other except for a few words I could make out. Then all the sudden the bitch erupted into chaos as mothafucka's went toe to toe throwing punches. In the matter of a minute the whole cell exploded into a brawl. Except for my ass who wasn't on one side or the other. This shit was like a fucking movie. I stood up watching.

A whistle from the hall caught my attention. Javier was standing right by the entrance to the cell.

The shit hit me, all this was set up. It was time to make shit happen now. The small warning Javier told me this morning meant that Juan had followed through and the backing from the CJNG was getting me the fuck out of here sooner than I thought.

Without hesitation, I hurried the fuck up over to the hall where he was standing. One of the guards looked my way and then turned back around like he never saw my ass. This whole fucking place was monitored with 24 hour surveillance, everywhere except the damn showers. But as we passed another guard who ignored seeing us while we rushed down the corridor, I knew without a doubt they were all in on this shit.

It was crazy as hell how far the cartels reach was here in Mexico. Back in the states bosses had pull, but prison breaks weren't common like here. In this prison everything was state of the art with a whole lot of fucking gates, cells and locks. But every single one was unlocked on our way.

Javier led me down 3 flights to the bottom level and then to the kitchen. He went around to the back, behind the serving line, where the food was prepared. I followed his ass to the very back of the kitchen area past the walk in fridge and pantry to a back door. He knocked twice on the door that looked like it was used for loading.

All this was fucking amazing. But I wasn't gonna question a mothafuckin' thing. I could ask questions later from the outside. Fuck that.

The door opened from the other side and another guard held the shit open. No words were spoken, but Javier nodded and I stepped through feeling the fresh night air on my face. The guard let the door fall shut again behind me as I came across. It was almost pitch black with the stars and moon giving the only light to be able to see. But I knew exactly what was next.

There was a big ass food delivery truck backed up to the loading dock. The back of the truck was up and the shit was already running, ready to go. It was only half full since they probably just brought a delivery in. I stepped across the small gap between the platform and the truck and went all the way into the bitch. Squatting down behind a pile of boxes filled with cartons of milk and produce.

The bitch was cold, but not unbearable. Before I knew it, the truck doors closed and complete darkness surrounded me with a big ass smile plastered on my face. A nigga was on his way home, ready to handle shit once and for all. I had 6 months of planning my next moves, making vows about a whole lot of shit.

Ready to see my bitch, my sister, my team and come back ten times stronger than I left. No more of this bullshit going back and forth putting me on my toes. Niggas were gonna pay.

Jolie

Since the sitter was already watching my babies, I went ahead and scheduled a hair appointment. My shit was out of control and I needed some help with it. I usually was the one out of me and Nya that played the beautician role, but I wanted something new. Something different for the first time. I normally rocked my natural loose curls that I got from my mixed bag of genetics that came from who the hell knew where. Some creole mixed with whatever else Beyoncé was talking about. That was me.

I went to the only shop that was official on this side of town and slid into a chair waiting for one of the stylists to finish up. I didn't know any of the women who worked in here, but when I walked in I got the feeling that they knew of me. That shit didn't surprise me, since it was known all over this area that I was Saint's sister. I just didn't do shit these days, or hell, even back before all the drama of the past year. Saint made sure my ass was on a short leash and not into shit.

I did recognize one of the women sitting in a chair at the back of the place as someone I went to high school with. We weren't ever close, so it wasn't worth speaking up right now. I chose to go through my emails and see if there was any new shit from the accountant.

As far as the business end of my brother's organization everything was legal, besides the money laundered into the restaurant and strip club. But the accountants didn't know that shit. So all communication was done digitally, over the phone or through emails.

"Jolie." One of the hairdressers stepped to the front and called my name.

I followed behind her and took a seat in her chair. I got real nervous all of the sudden. I usually just trimmed my own damn hair. But it was time for a change. I was becoming a new woman and my hair was just another part of the transformation for me. I wanted to surprise the hell out of Drew tonight too. I unconsciously began to blush and when I looked up in the mirror in front of me, meeting the stylist's eyes the shit got worse. It was like I was caught thinking about Drew, even though I wasn't.

"So what you wanna do hunny? Your hair is so beautiful."

"I'm just ready for something new. As long as you don't leave me looking like Tamar, then do your thing. I put my trust in your hands." I was giving this bitch a lot of confidence.

43

She better not fuck up my shit. We would see. After following her and having her wash and fully dry my hair I was right back in the seat turned around, hearing scissors cut through my curls. I saw the floor filling up below my feet, only making me more anxious. Finally, she asked if I would be okay with some color. I reassured her to do what she thought would look good. After another hour, another wash/dry, it was finally time to see whether I made a good decision or not.

When she turned me around, I for real put my hands to my mouth barely recognizing myself. Damn it was like I was grown up sexy as hell, even dressed in a track suit. I knew my bitch was gonna love it and Drew was gonna eat this shit up. Hell, that wasn't the only thing he was gonna be eating later. I loved getting my pussy ate, so he better get used to it off the bat.

My hair was now shoulder length dyed a burgundy red with dark roots, my curls still intact. Despite struggling with confidence I was really feeling this new look. In a lot of ways I more reserved except with the people I was close to. But in the bedroom all that went out the window.

I paid the woman and left an extra hundred for tip. She deserved the shit. Walking out of the salon I really felt like a new woman from head to toe. I was ready for this. This new life I wanted.

I hurried back home ready to see my children and spend some time with them. This would be the first full night since I brought BJ home and Joy was born that they would stay overnight without me. Both of them loved Nya, and she did the most spoiling their asses. So I knew they were in good hands. She needed the practice anyway since my nephew was due any time now. It was nice to have family you could count on.

I made it home in a few minutes and let the babysitter leave after paying her. She was in college to become a teacher and a regular life saver whenever I had to handle business on weekends or evenings. I went in the living room ready to play and cool it with the kids but both their butts were asleep looking real comfortable. BJ on my usual side of the couch laid up, like he had been waiting for me. Joy was in her swing, swaying slowly with a peaceful expression on her face.

I walked over to her first and placed a soft kiss on her head rubbing my hand over her thick ass head of hair being sure not to wake her. Then slid the throw blanket over BJ and kicked off my shoes. I might as well take a nap with them. Who knows how much sleep I was gonna get tonight?

Hours later, I was seated across from Drew dining at Saint's restaurant downtown. I loved this place. Not just because it was a part of my family, or because I was proud as hell of my big brother, but because the food was fire. The shit was so good. Just like everything else it was nothing but the best with Saint.

I took the last bite of my 10 oz. steak enjoying the savory juices it was marinated in. When I felt Drew's eyes watching me. I looked across the table and our eyes locked. His dark eyes were intense, glazed over from the Cush he smoked on the way here, but they were speaking to me. And that wasn't the damn weed.

He was ready to fuck. I made sure to take my time and open my mouth wider being extra seductive when I licked my lips after. He reached across the table with the linen napkin in his hand,

"That good?" He asked in his deep voice, making my pussy purr.

Drew had his own accent. Not quite the same as a typical nigga out the streets but far from a typical white boy either. He was cut form his own damn cloth. I had never met anyone like him, from his looks to his demeanor. It was all genuine and he was about to be all mine.

46

"Yeah, it was good bae, but I'm ready for something better." I answered him, keeping my eyes on his and reaching under the table with one of my hands, resting it on his knee.

"He dropped a few bills on the table and stood up pulling me with him.

"Let's go."

On the way back to his place, it was eerily quiet even with his music playing filling the empty space. Doubts started to fill my head but I pushed them all away. I wanted this.

Sooner than I thought, we pulled into his spot that he kept out here in New Orleans. It wasn't nowhere near the best or worst place in downtown New Orleans. Right on the water on the 10th floor, he had a good ass view of the river overlooking the West Bank where I resided.

But we weren't here for the view. I followed him inside, up the elevator and the moment we got to his door he turned around. Drew had been holding my hand the whole way while walking but kept his words to nothing more than a few here and there.

When he turned around he swung me around, back up against the door to his condo. I had already been here a few times, but nothing like this was on the agenda. He towered over me, all muscles and that sexy ass strong jaw shaded with a slight beard. He picked my ass up with my back braced against the door now. I wrapped my legs around his waist and felt his hard dick on my abdomen. Damn it was hard. And it was big.

I had never been with a white man before. So I didn't know what to expect, but Drew had a way of making me forget about his skin color. He was simply hands down sexy as hell in his own damn lane, like no other man I had met before.

He bent forward kissing me deep then pulling back enough to lay more on my neck, alternating between sucking and kissing. My pussy was leaking. I was ready to get inside and finally get some dick. It had really been a whole damn year.

"Damn your skin tastes good as fuck." He whispered in my ear.

Somehow he managed to unlock and open the door while going to work on my mouth and neck. I was in trouble. He was so damn slick.

He carried me inside. Then walked me over to the island in between the living room and kitchen. Setting me down and pulling away, finally breaking the contact of his lips on my skin.

"What are you doing to me?" I asked as a chill went through my body.

He spread my legs apart and pulled my knit dress up. I raised up enough for him to bring it completely over my head in the process.

Then he started kissing all over my body, unsnapping my bra from the back and paying attention to my breasts swirling his tongue over each of my chocolate drop nipples. Everything he was doing was affecting me to the max. My body shook and I held him by the shoulders for dear life. It had been so long since I had been touched intimately and every part of me was more sensitive like it was my first time. Minus not knowing what the hell was in store or what to do.

Drew backed away again this time kicking off his shoes and unbuckling his belt. I stared on admiring my man. He was fine as hell, abs chiseled out like a Greek God and his tattoos across his chest added to his thug appeal. Looking down below the waistline of his boxer briefs my breath caught in my chest for a minute. He was big as hell like I thought from the feel of it. I was curious and turned on. I wanted to see the shit.

I leaned forward causing my breasts to plump together more. I was already big chested with Double D's, thick everywhere except my small waist. His eyes stayed trained on mine, while I reached out and grabbed his dick through the thin fabric and began stroking it, feeling his long and thick shaft. Hopefully it fit.

I wasn't used to getting dicked down. Buck had been about the same size. Fuck, I shook the thought of him away and let my grip go leaning back on the palms of my hand, resting back against the cold marble countertop.

Drew hesitated, he must have sensed my mental retreat.

"We ain't gotta do this..."

I cut him off by pulling him all the way into me. His body pressed against mine.

"Nah, I want this. I want you bae. I'm ready."

He didn't waste another minute as he gripped my thighs again, this time rougher and then backed away again. I was about to ask him what the fuck he was doing, but this man went and picked up one of the chairs at the table and brought it over to the counter right in front of me. He sat his ass down and held onto my legs again. I already missed the warmth from his hands on my body. Damn.

"Your skin tastes good as fuck. I bet your pussy sweeter. You're my dessert."

He brought my body forward partly off the counter, ass in the air. He tore my G-string thong off and dove in face first. Instantly applying pressure from his tongue on my pussy lips, working his way to my opening. I draped my legs over his shoulders and leaned back more working my pussy all on his face letting him get all the juices he wanted.

He brought his hands up and gripped my ass hard, sending me over the damn edge. The next thing I knew my body was bouncing on his mouth faster. I screamed out his name back to back, as my cum exploded in his mouth. He didn't stop though, this mothafucka latched onto my clit afterwards and kept going until my body finally slowed down and my breathing got calmer. Reading my body and reaction, like he knew exactly what I was feeling.

"Damn, bae. I want to taste you too." I finally said once my heartrate slowed down.

"I got you this time. Now bring that fat ass here." He stood up and I attempted to walk over to him after jumping off the counter onto the ground below. But this man had really fucked up my body. My legs weren't cooperating and I half stumbled, trying to walk. I cummed quick and hard, after waiting so long to be with a man. I was fucked up off him eating my pussy alone.

He stepped towards me and flipped me over his shoulder like I didn't weight a thing. I was always self-conscious of my weight but he always complimented my figure and now that I was completely naked his didn't seem to mind my fuller figure either.

My head was against his back, hair all in my face upside down, with him gripping my ass nice and firm. He walked through another door into his bedroom.

"I can walk, Drew! I promise, you can put me down."

"I know I fucked up your head girl, you need the break trust me. 'Cus this dick is about to really fuck you up."

I couldn't say anything in response. He dropped me down on his massive bed. I turned around as he was finishing taking off his boxers, Fuck. He was so sexy. His dick was pointing at me, standing at attention and I was ready for all of him.

I scooted up on the bed to the pillows and laid back, massaging my breasts and moving one hand down to play with my clit, giving my man a show he could appreciate.

He got between my legs and kissed the side of my knees, then spread them further apart so they were as far gapped as they could go comfortably. He put the tip of his dick right at my entrance.

"This means you're mine. Ain't no going back." He didn't wait for a response. He wasn't asking. He was telling. But I was okay with that. I wanted him to be mine the same way. It was time we became official and say fuck whoever didn't like that shit. He was my future and I was his.

Saint

Crossing into California after the escape was one of the best fucking feelings. That was 3 days ago. And for the past two of them I had been going hard as hell in Houston doing my own fucking surveillance on shit out here to see what the hell had been going on while I was away.

That wasn't the only reason I waited and stayed put out here instead of rushing home to see my family. I also needed to catch up with those two bitches that were with the nigga Julius. Like I said, I wasn't leaving any loose ends anymore. I wouldn't be able to sleep at night knowing they were free and clear after putting the shit in motion, causing me to be away for the past six months and causing shit to go bad with Nya. I was making moves against Pedro but that shit was gonna take some time to get the go-ahead from the plug. Like it or not, I had to be more patient on that front.

I did end up dialing Nya's number to see if she would pick up. I hadn't been in direct contact with anyone, not even Juan since the coyote's smuggled me across the border and dropped me off. The man driving gave me a duffle bag with few thousand in cash, an ID that looked exactly like my real shit if I didn't know better, a cell phone, and a new outfit.

I changed right away and ended up buying a new pair of kicks with the money. I knew Juan left the shit for me and set all this up. I would owe him for this shit down the road. Even with his ass there was always a catch.

It took me almost an hour to get the fucking nerve up to actually dial the shit. I wasn't pussy about nothing, but when it came to the possibility of Nya not being alive or my seed not making it, that shit fucked with my damn soul.

After she picked up, I hung up the phone. I knew it was her. Nya sounded just like I remembered and the attitude she caught almost caused me to say some shit. But I didn't want her to worry more or try and convince me to come home. I needed to take care of business first.

Drew apparently was out of town. I assumed in New Orleans for the first couple of days when I showed up. But as I sat at the bus stop near the downtown spot that the operation moved out of, I saw him pull up to the curb. Yeah, my boy was official as hell now, looking like a solid ass boss. That could only mean that he had been successful in holding shit down while I was away. I never doubted him for a minute.

I stood up and walked across the street catching up with him before he went inside. I tapped him on the shoulder firm enough to get his attention. Causing him to draw his piece and have it pointed in my face within a blink of an eye. Yeah that was my mothafuckin' man, staying on his toes at all times. He shouldn't have let a nigga get up close to him though. He needed to watch that shit.

Drew had a look of pure surprise for a minute. It was still early as hell being only 7 o'clock in the morning, so I needed to make this shit quick. Too many eyes and ears would only slow me down. I wanted this to be done within the next few hours.

"Damn, mane." He broke out in a genuine smile and put his shit away. "Bout to get your brains blown out."

"Stay on your toes bruh, that could've been over with before you knew it." I patted him on the shoulder and then started walking over to the passenger side of his car.

He got the message that I wanted to talk in there instead of out in the open and walked back over to his ride. Once we were sitting inside, I got straight to the shit.

"First things first, how's my family?" I asked trying to judge his demeanor when listening to see if he was gonna hold shit back or be a hundred.

Trust was still something that I struggled with even with the people closest to me. Family issues left me fucked up in the head that way.

"Shit's good. Nya and the baby are good. I woke up that night and got her to the hospital in time from you yelling the way you did. The shit paid off. She's about to drop the baby any day now. Jolie... She's straight. Taking care of BJ and she has a daughter. Your niece, Joy." He said pulling out his phone and then handing it to me showing me a picture.

The shit was nice to see, but he was holding back when it came to my sister. Why the hell would he have her and my niece's pictures in his phone? Before I checked him about it, he continued what he was saying, "Look, Saint. Me and Jolie are together now. It happened over time and you wasn't here to run shit by. So I'm bringing it to you now out of respect."

Damn what was it with my sister and my right hands. I shook my head and then asked, "So if I say end the shit, you'll respect me on that?" I wanted to see his reaction to that shit.

"To be honest, I would have to decline. I don't want to be your enemy. You're my boss and my partna, but I can't let her go. I love her."

There it was. That I could respect. If he would have given any other answer, then I wasn't with the shit. She needed someone willing to go against all odds to take care of her. Not some fuck boy who wouldn't go to bat when shit went sour. I didn't like to think about my sister with any man. But Drew was better than most and who else would I rather have her with. At least I knew his character. Both Jolie and Drew were grown and deserved to be happy. I wish I had the opportunity to have this conversation with Buck before he got taken down.

"You're good." I finally answered. "Just don't fuck her over, ya heard meh." I ended with. "Now that that's out the way, I need your gun and for you to hook me up with a rental car with a big ass trunk. I gotta take care of those bitches today so I can get the fuck outa Houston and head home."

He handed me his revolver without hesitation. This was why I fucked with him. He was genuine and always fucking dependable.

"Anything else? I'm with you bruh."

"I got this one. Good lookin' out fam. Do me a favor and keep this shit between us. I don't want Jolie or Nya to know until they see me face to face."

I hopped out of the ride after slapping hands with my partna and tucking the heat in the back of my pants. It was time to take out these bitches and put at least part of this shit behind us for good.

Thinking about Nya was what got me through all the months away with a sane mind. I was already a little crazy, but knowing I needed to do whatever it took to see her again kept me from ending up in that Mexican prison for a life sentence behind not giving a fuck.

Knowing she was fine and the baby was about to be here made me feel like it was all worth it. First thing I was doing after this shit today, was laying up with my bitch and getting some pussy.

Nya

"Mmmmmm"

The dream I had over and over was replaying again, I always was aware that it was a dream as if I was awake watching as an outer body experience, unable to do anything to stop it. This time shit changed up. Saint was sliding up under the covers coming to bed, similar to the many nights he just got in from the streets.

He found his way up under my silk nightgown and rested his hands on top of my protruding stomach as gentle as ever with his mouth close to my pussy, before sticking his tongue deep inside me. Swirling it around against my walls that were tight from even the slightest penetration. I spread my legs wider, giving him easier access, wanting more, needing more. I never wanted this feeling to stop.

The shit felt too real. The thought of it being just another dream clouded the feelings the memory of my fucking soul mate brought in this vivid dream. I tried to wake myself up.

Damnit wake the fuck up NyAsia. He's gone. Get it together. I thought to myself, finally able to come back to reality, opening my eyes in the pitch black room.

I wasn't one of those bitches that could sleep with light or noise. I liked the serenity and quietness of a dark room while I slept. Those nights Saint unintentionally kept the big ass flat screen TV on left me with a bad ass headache the next day.

But being awake from the dream, looking around, seeing nothing fucked with my head more. I was still feeling a very real man between my legs under the cover. I screamed out, and kicked like hell pushing myself more into the headboard. Who the fuck was in my bed?

I gathered my composure fast as hell. Reaching under the pillow I pulled out Saint's Glock. I always kept some heat under me while I slept these days. This was the life of a gangsta's bitch. Nobody was catching me slipping again if I could help it.

I aimed the tool straight ahead, still unable to make out the figure. The covers were completely off of me from the kicking and thrashing I did, leaving me exposed and chilled from the air conditioned room. I still held the piece straight ahead with steady hands.

"You picked the wrong bitch to fuck with."

I spoke loud and clear with an unwavering coldness. Whoever thought they could come into my damn home and try some rape shit with me was dead ass wrong. Pregnant or not, enemy of Saint or not, I was gonna be just fine and could handle myself. This mothafucka had misjudged me in the worst way.

I leaned over, changing my grip to one hand, still ready to pull the trigger. Then switched on the lamp light from the bedside table. The minute the dim light shone in the room, I dropped the weapon, hands shaking.

How the fuck? Could this really be happening, or was I losing my damn mind?

"Damn shawty, you missed your nigga I see." Saint easily said with a smile on his lips.

At this point the tears were falling from my eyes and my entire body was shaking. I missed the man standing before me more than I thought possible. He was my entire world and my heart broke being without him. Now seeing him, standing here brought out all the emotions I was holding back.

"Oh my God! Baby, I'm so sorry. I didn't know it was you. Why didn't you say something?" I attempted to stand up out of bed and make my way to him.

He came over to me instead, reaching out and placing his palms on the tops of my shoulders, resting them there. Sending another chill down my body. Like a jolt of electricity, making my pussy respond along with the rest of me.

I looked up at him standing above me with his eyes roaming all over my body and finally landing on my stomach. He lowered his hand and rested it on top, like he had been doing when he started eating my pussy a few minutes ago.

"How's my son?"

"HE'S good! How are you? Where have you been? I missed you so much." I let all this shit fly out of my mouth one after the other, causing tears to fall again. I was only weak behind one thing and that was my damn family. Otherwise, I didn't cry. I didn't wear my heart on my sleeve. They brought out the best and worst in me.

"Shhhhh. We got time to talk 'bout all that bullshit. But right now I want to finish what the fuck I started and taste my bitch. I'm digging up in those guts, feeling MY pussy."

Shit, my nigga didn't have to say shit else. I was ready, been ready for months. Saint began taking off the rest of his clothes, his boxers and wife beater. Seeing his body in the flesh still had the same effect. He was like a work of art made just for me.

He reached down again and began pinching and rolling his thumb and fingers over my nipples, making them hard as fuck.

I let my hands roam over Saint's body, grabbing his big ass dick with my outstretched hand in return. It was hard and pointing in my face. I wanted to taste him too. I stroked his dick up and down with a firm grip. Then looked up at him forming my mouth into an O, moving my lips over his dick.

I started to work my tongue back and forth creating more spit and less friction. Then relaxed my throat and went down further. The shit caused me to choke. It had been so damn long, I had to get used to pleasing him again. But even through the gagging, I wanted more. Sucking Saint's dick turned me on just as much as him. I loved taking care of my nigga and having him in the palm of my hand. Saint hardly ever gave up control, so being able to take charge made shit that much better.

"That's that shit I like. Handle your dick bae."

I stopped fucking around and began suctioning my jaws in and out, working my mouth as I slid my hand up and down at the same pace. Saint reached around the back of my head pulling my hair back roughly, gripping a handful of it, not too hard and not too soft. Keeping his hand on the back of my head still looking down at me.

Then I really fucked him up, letting his dick slide down my throat as far as it could go, humming on him. I let up and sucked his shaft, putting my mouth to work faster than I ever had before. This made his ass go in a damn frenzy. His dick got even harder and his breathing picked up. I loved the shit.

"If you been with another nigga, I'm killing you." He said serious, between breaths. His grip on the back of my head got tighter.

He pushed my head down more and took control while his dick pulsed and warm cum shot out inside my mouth. I drank up every drop then eased back off his dick, placing kisses along the side of it where the saliva was drying up. He let go of the back of my head.

"Saint you know I'm all yours." I said reassuring him standing up from the side of the bed.

He wrapped his arms around me and gripped my ass.

"I know you ain't crazy. But damn, where the fuck that come from?" He asked seriously.

"I just wanted to see if you liked it? I love sucking your dick and tasting you." I answered just as serious back without any shame.

Shit, my nigga wanted to know and I would always be honest. I didn't mind him talking shit and being rough either. I trusted him with my life. He could fuck me or make love to me however he wanted, whenever he wanted.

"Oh yeah?" He said not looking for me to say anything back.

Turning me around and pressing down on the upper half of my back. He ran his strong hand down the curve of my frame all the way to the crack of my ass. Being so pregnant and my stomach being ready to pop, this was probably the best position to have sex. Saint knew exactly what the hell he was doing.

"I missed you shawty."

He started rubbing my pussy with his fingers feeling the outside lips, with his thumb still in my crack. My body was tingling on edge, wound up already wanting a release.

I felt his warm breath on my pussy. I bent forward more, resting my palms on the bed in front of me, tooting my ass up and spreading my legs wider in anticipation. I wanted his touch, everything he had to give right now.

Saint extended his hands on either side of my ass cheeks, opening me up for him from the back. All out exposed, so my nigga could eat the fuck out of my pussy. I didn't give a fuck.

His tongue moved back and forth causing vibrations to rack through my inner most part, flicking it in and out fast. I backed

66

my ass up into his mouth more. He slowed down and began really making love to my pussy with his mouth. Sucking nice and slow, with pressure all over from my clit to my ass. Then went in further finding my clit.

He finger fucked me, moving his two fingers in and out my pussy repeatedly while his mouth assaulted me. All I could do was take what he was doing. I couldn't move, couldn't form a thought, just feel him. He was everywhere, invading my inner most parts.

I clenched the bed sheets and finally popped my pussy, as my cum gushed out in his mouth. I rode that shit out while my nigga took his time catching all my juices.

By the time he was done eating my pussy, I was tired and out of breath. His ass knew what the fuck he was doing to me. So he wasted no time dropping his big ass dick in me, making my breath catch in my throat before I screamed out.

"Ahhhhhh," I couldn't help show the pain in my voice.

I felt like I was being ripped apart. It had been so long and he was so big. He stopped moving. Like it was our first time all over again.

"I got you. Open up for me." Like always his words were music to my ears and my body's objections melted away.

He slid his dick all the way in, touching the base of my pussy and putting pressure on my cervix. Deep, stretching me wide, completely filled I began twisting my hips grinding on my man. This was everything. The feeling of his long slow strokes made me bolder. So I picked up the pace.

That was all it took. He pulled out and helped me back off the bed more, easing my head down on the mattress instead of my hands. I was bent over further, ass in the air on my tiptoes. He grabbed both my hands, and held them behind my back, with my cheek pressed against the bed, head turned to the side as he entered me again.

He entered me slowly this time. But it didn't matter, I couldn't fucking move, couldn't twerk on his dick, nothing. Saint was in control now, having his way with me with me like he wanted.

"Let me feel that shit." He said, right before I cummed again, the pressure from my release trying to push him out. "Yeah, that pussy got some power, but this dick got more."

He wasn't lying. He continued to hold my hands tight and laid back to back deep strokes on me, causing me to come up on my tiptoes higher.

"Saint, oh My God, I love you, shit!" I needed to let him know how this shit felt.

Before I couldn't say shit else. Because after I let the words out, he went faster. The bed bouncing hard from the impact, digging in me further than I thought possible. All at once he stopped and held still, before his dick jumped and we cummed together. I screamed out and even heard a small grunt from his ass.

Damn, I was completely unable to move, from fear that I would fall over. Saint must have realized how fucked up his dick had me. Even though I knew my pussy had his ass weak too, He lifted me up like I wasn't 9 months pregnant and laid me on the bed.

Was this all real? I couldn't help the thought creeping back in my mind. I had wished for this to happen over and over again for months and now Saint was here giving me the best dick of my life. Was I really this lucky? Did God really look out for me like this?

I still had so many unanswered questions as to where he was and what happened to him. But all that mattered was that Saint was back. In just the last hour, my heart was filled and I was complete. Anything else didn't matter right now. I drifted off to sleep more peaceful than I ever remember being able to. I prayed that when I woke up Saint was still next to me, and I hadn't gone completely crazy imagining the damn whole thing.

Saint

After last night, I was finally feeling on top of the world, where the fuck I should have been this whole fucking year with the love of my life by my side. Instead I was running back and forth between here and Houston, trying to catch all the mothafucka's who were after me and my girl. That shit was coming to an end once and for all.

Seeing Nya and knowing my seed was good was the best it got for a nigga like me. But handling these bitches would be a good ass feeling too. I originally planned on taking care of them myself. But I wanted to let Nya in on the shit. This way she would get some kind of closure and we could finally move on to better days ahead of us.

The other shit with Pedro was already in motion and his days were numbered. Next month the mothafucka wouldn't be breathing. If the cartel didn't come through for me on the hit, then I was saying fuck it and going after him myself without their approval even if it meant my death. I couldn't let him live.

Soon it would be no more looking in the past or watching over our shoulders. Not to say some shit wouldn't come up in the future. But we damn sure deserved a break for a couple years from the bullshit. Being in the streets would always bring enemies and peace would come and go. But me and Nya hadn't even had a full month without some mothafuckas coming against us.

My bitch was a cold ass killer as much as I was, so I knew she would appreciate the opportunity to take care of the women who tried to fuck with her. I almost reconsidered seeing how close she was to dropping my son. Any day now, he would be here. I was looking forward to that shit to the fullest. Passing my name down and knowing that my blood flowed in his veins was real legacy shit.

I didn't tell Nya where we were headed. She tried getting hints from my ass before we left. Asking what she should wear. I just told her to be comfortable. Hell, a mothafucka could murder a nigga in anything. All she had to do was pull the trigger. I couldn't wait to see the look on her face when she realized what she was in for.

We turned into a drive of one of the old abandoned buildings off Thayer St. The thing about our operation that set us apart from the downtown and uptown crews was that we didn't operate all our business out of one location. Being on the West Bank gave us a reprieve from some of the shit that went on closer to the center of the city. We could move differently over here.

This place along with some of the other closed down buildings were where we did our hands on work. We switched spots up and kept the bitches secure. Unless some shit came up out of the blue we were set. The niggas on my team were the only eyes for several blocks out.

If 12 rolled up on the shit we would be warned at least 15 minutes before they arrived, giving us enough time to bounce and not catch any real heat. There might be product left behind, but they wouldn't find any evidence to pin that shit on me or the niggas in the organization. The real authorized shit was on lock over here. How those niggas across the bridge handled their product and dough was their burden not mine. I lived and breathed for this shit. The West Bank was the best fuckin' bank.

After unlocking the chain from the gate, I got back in my ride and pulled into a parking spot close to the front of the old Cargo building. Parking behind one of the rusted out beat up cars, partially overgrown by grass and weeds. Nya looked at me. I knew she was wondering what the hell we were doing out here. There was still a lot about my business in the streets she didn't know about even with her taking control of certain parts while I was gone.

"I got a surprise for you shawty."

"Why are you always playing boy? It's too damn early. You're lucky you laid the dick on me so good. Otherwise I would be cursing your ass out for real. Dragging me out of bed at 8:00 in the damn morning, pffff... What the hell is wrong with you? And why the hell is this surprise all the way out here Saint?" She asked, talking shit even though she said she wasn't. That attitude was as thick as her accent when she was irritated.

I chuckled, not saying shit in response. Instead I opened the car door and got out of the whip. Nya followed along, like I knew she would. She was stubborn as hell but not as stubborn as me. She would find out soon enough what her surprise was.

We walked up the loading ramp that was once used for trucks picking up cargo. Then I reached down and pulled up the garage-like door. After Nya stepped behind me into the large warehouse, I pulled the shit back down.

Normally, this place was shrouded in complete darkness since there wasn't any electricity in the bitch. But I had portable lanterns hung off the building's metal frame, making the shit light the fuck up. You could see perfectly once your eyes adjusted to the shit.

The two women were hidden underneath a blanket in a cage set up in the corner. Both their asses slept like that. Fuck 'em. They shouldn't have come after my family. That shit cost them their lives. They had a choice like everybody else not to fuck with me, but they chose not to. That shit was on them.

I wasn't into fucking with innocent women or children. The way my team moved was different than that sloppy shit that left babies and bystanders dead for no fucking reason. I only went after mothafuckas when I had to. This shit was more than personal this time, it was business. Setting niggas up and the bullshit drama caused by these two hoes was over with today.

"Okay, why are we here bae?" Nya's tone sweetened up some.

I kissed her and then turned back around. I would rather show then tell her. So I walked over the cage and opened it, uncovering the women. They both looked a fucking mess. Two days with no change of clothes, pissing and shitting on themselves would do that. They were as good as dead anyway. Some niggas would have been a lot harder on them and done all types of shit. But the only thing I wanted was for them to be dead, fuck all that other shit.

Nya walked right up to the bitches and I fell back letting her take control. She stared down at them then glanced over her shoulder at me. There was the look I was expecting. The look of a down ass bitch ready to handle business. There was also some other shit there, more than what I expected to see.

"You brought me presents." Nya said in an ice cold tone.

"These bitches fucked with you and my son. Handle yo' buinsess, ya heard meh."

"Payback's a bitch..." She started to say then became quiet.

She got a hold of the younger girl first, the one I fucked. The hoe who started this shit. I couldn't even remember her name now. Nya tore off the duct tape covering her mouth. She tried to scream, but only a raspy noise came out instead.

"This the bitch that wanted you all for herself bae... Yeah, you hoe! You thought you were gonna get rid of me?" The girl shook her head no, her eyes darting back and forth between me and Nya. "I'm still standing bitch, still having MY nigga's baby, still here. And where are you?!" Nya asked.

Then without warning Nya pulled her arm back and swung on her. A quick punch to the nose making the girl's shit bust open and blood leak out. Nya didn't flinch from the impact, but I knew her shit would be swollen later. I didn't want her doing too much being pregnant. But throwing a few punches wouldn't hurt nothing. She was solid all the way around.

Nya finished getting her anger out by kicking the girl in the face, using the wall to hold her balance. Anyone looking on would have thought this shit was crazy since she was pregnant as hell. But retribution was a mothafucka and Nya needed to get her aggression out.

Next, Nya stepped over to the older woman. She was bigger than the other one and had sat up, hands still tied behind her back, tape covering her mouth. She didn't have the same look of fear the other girl had. Nya didn't bother pulling the shit off her mouth. Instead she continued to talk to me and no one in particularly at the same time.

"And this evil bitch... Bae, can you believe this is my aunt? The same one that tried to break me." She turned her attention back on the woman. "After all you did to me, it's by my hands that your fucked up life will end. Even God will be smiling down watching me kill yo' ass. This shit's for all the girls you had raped."

The woman finally had the look I was waiting for; Fear. She knew it was over for her. Hearing Nya say all that shit set a fire in me too. This was her aunt, the one who let niggas rape her when she was still a damn kid. The one who was supposed to be her fucking family and take care of her. I handed my gun to Nya.

She reached out and looked at me one more time before turning that shit on her aunt with a blank stare. Then lowered the tool, aimed it directly between the bitch's eyes, and squeezed the trigger. She turned the shit on the other girl next and let another one off, hitting her in the head. Both their bodies slumped over. Nya tucked the heat in the back of her leggings like that shit was gonna work.

I pulled her body into mine wrapping my arms around her waist, taking the gun out of her pants and letting my hands linger on her ass gripping the mothafucka. Seeing her take care of these two had my dick hard, ready to fuck. She faced the shit with her head held high and did what the fuck she needed to do to keep herself and our family safe.

Nya reached out and stroked my dick through my pants. Sharing a deep ass kiss like we always did when shit got real, like it was life or death. With this life, it always was. Every minute we had together was the best a nigga like me could hope for.

Jolie

After the out of this world 2 days of being laid up with my new man, I was still trying to recover. My sleep was completely out of whack. Having a newborn and a toddler didn't help with getting any extra shut eye either. Not that I would have it any other way, but after going so long without getting dicked down a bitch really had to recover.

I was finally starting to feel normal again. This morning I made my usual cup of green tea added some honey and sat back on the couch, relaxing and scrolling though Instagram. I preferred this to any other social media because it was less personal and more entertaining.

As I sat back enjoying the comfort of the oversized pillows and soft couch, a new text notification came through with a message from Nya. She wanted to meet up again today at the house downtown. I expected to hear back from her today or tomorrow about the shit we were dealing with concerning business.

Nya went ahead and put in a phone call to set up an official sit down with the other bosses in the city. This was a big step for us. It was the first time we would be the face of the West Bank in a meeting of this magnitude. Instead of it being Saint or Buck we would be there making moves.

The downtown boss Marlo knew what the hell he was doing. Him trying to change things up wasn't just testing our operation, it was some real disrespectful shit to Saint. Trying to take advantage of us, going back on their original agreement because Saint wasn't here. Nya was hoping her friendship with Ron could help our positions and that he would side with us. Having the support of Uptown would make us more solid. If he wasn't with it, everything could fall apart and everything my brother worked so hard for could be lost.

All because some nigga didn't want to do business with women. I bet a lot of fucking money it had to do with more of who we were than a legit business reason why this man was testing us. Fuck men!

I mean except my man, my brother and my adopted son. I was a feminist at heart and hated to be thought of as less than. Most of the time a woman was ten times smarter and could handle way more. I had to admit though, some of this street shit wasn't for me. That was where Nya came in. It didn't matter that she was a woman. She was as good as any other nigga running shit and she had just started.

When I first woke up I called Drew, making my day start off right. This man put a permanent smile on my face. He was opening up my heart more and more. It amazed me how comfortable I was with him and how important he already was to me.

I finished my drink and washed the morning dishes, drying and putting them away before going down the hall to take a shower and finish getting ready for the day. Since it was the middle of the week, the kids were going to daycare instead of the sitter. I liked for them to be watched here whenever possible. But Malaysia, my sitter had classes during the week. So if needed, I took them to the best day care in town.

I damn sure couldn't take them with me into potentially dangerous situations. Even though nobody technically knew the house downtown belonged to us, you could never be a hundred percent sure about any damn thing. That was another thing I didn't like about the streets. They had a way of following you home and taking away your peace of mind. I was accustomed to it for so long, but having kids now, it was a whole other thing.

I got my clothes ready for the day. A pair of light faded jeans with rips in the knees and a burgandy red fitted T. The color matched the same deep red of my dyed hair, more of an eggplant now. I loved my new look and was still shocked whenever I saw my reflection in the mirror. My confidence was at an all-time high. It didn't hurt that Drew found a million ways to tell me how much he loved the way I looked with and without my clothes on. I was still shy, but he helped me realize more of my good features.

I took a quick shower before heading out to see Nya. I had forgotten that she hadn't seen me since I got the new hairstyle. My head had been completely wrapped up in my own life over the past couple days, which was unlike me. So on my way to the house downtown I called her. She picked up, sounding real funny. There was something different about her voice.

"Hey hunny." She answered, with a light and excited voice.

Knowing Nya like I did, it was still way too early for her to be this bright and cheery. It was already around ten o'clock, but my girl was the last person in the world to talk happy shit before noon. Being pregnant only amplified her attitude in the morning. So hopefully she had some good news for me.

"What's up girl? Something good from the sound of your voice." I said.

"Oh, well... you know I'm just glad the doctor finally agreed to induce me Tuesday if this damn baby don't get the hell up out of here on his own." She said now changing her tune, and sounding more like the Nya I was used to hearing. Yeah something was up, but I left it alone.

"Leave my nephew alone, you know he's gotta do shit his way just like his daddy, it's only right." I joked.

"Mmmhhhm, you're right about that. JUST LIKE HIS DADDY." There it was again, her funny acting ass. Oh well. I would grill her at the house in a few minutes.

"I'm 'bout to stop and grab some food, I know your greedy ass wants something. So what's it gonna be today, baby mama?"

"Whatever! But since you asked, I will take some beignets and hot chocolate, please!"

"Your ass damn sure is pregnant, wanting hot chocolate. You know it's hot as hell today right?" I laughed right along with her ass.

Living in the South during the winter was up and down. One day the weather would be cold as hell and the next was like Spring.

"I got you of course, baby mama." I added.

I started calling her "baby mama" as soon as I visited her in the hospital and she woke up. I took care of her ass for the first couple months of her pregnancy after Saint was gone like she was my baby mama. Tending to her cravings and looking out for her, like she did me. That was why she called me "Ma J", the same as BJ did, whenever we joked around. She was a trip with it and people would look at us like we were crazy in public when they heard us talking. But ask either of us if we gave a fuck what anybody thought. Nope, not a single one.

I ended the call, stopping to the gas station a couple of blocks away from the usual pastry shop I went to whenever I came down this way. I got out of my Benz, taking a minute to look the bitch over and admire my first baby. I loved this car as much today as I did 4 years ago when Saint first surprised me with it. Everything that reminded me of my big brother was bittersweet right now. I missed his ass so damn much.

Deep in thought, I went ahead and started pumping gas with my eyes glued on the numbers running up on the pump screen. Not really focused on them until a familiar looking car pulled up on the opposite side of the pump. I couldn't figure out where I knew the car from until the bitch stepped out. Then I remembered where I saw the silver civic before.

Domonique stepped out of the car and looked over in my direction. Yup, she planned this shit and if she didn't before, she definitely saw my ass standing here before deciding to pull up. I glared back at her ass with the mean mug I meant to have. She still was an "ain't shit" bitch to me. She might look better than the last time I saw her. But she wasn't being a fucking mother to her son, so she wasn't shit.

The passenger door of the car opened and some nigga I had never seen before stood up. My first opinion of him was he was a bum ass nigga. What kind of grown ass man is gonna be riding around with this hoe first of all? He couldn't have been shit either because we were all too old for a man to still not have shit to his name and from the looks of him, he didn't have shit. But that was their business. They could just pretend like they didn't see my ass and go about their way as far as I was concerned. I stopped the gas from pumping prematurely and closed the cap.

Ignoring the couple I opened my car door back up. But I wasn't so lucky as to get out of there before the bitch had the nerve to say some shit.

"Wait, I know you see me over here. You're not even gonna tell me about my son? Bitch you better speak." She said bold as hell.

I looked in her direction, staring her down, "My Son's good". I wasn't about to waste my time with this dumb hoe.

She lost her son behind her own selfish actions. Wasn't no way she was gonna see him either with how she was obviously still out here living. She was worried about a man when she should have been doing everything in her power to get her shit together and be a fucking mother to her son. I knew her ass was still on that shit too, from how skinny and dull her sunken skin was. She might have tried to clean up her appearance, but an addict stuck out like a sore thumb.

I continued to close my car door, but her nigga stepped over and held the shit back so I wasn't able to close it.

"Bitch, what's the problem?" He caught an attitude trying to sound hard, but his ass was the exact opposite. Not a street nigga. More like a pussy trying to pretend. The most dangerous kind of no good nigga. He looked evil on top of it, without any damn sense behind the look he was giving me.

I wasn't about to play with either of them. I calmly pulled my gun out. The compact pistol was registered and legal. This was a stand your ground state, so I could easily pull the trigger and kill the man in front of me and it be justifiable. Using the law in my favor against these two like the sick white people do against innocent black kids.

I didn't know shit about the law until Nya came back and spewed out random facts to me. Not that I was uneducated. I mean I was a teacher, but law and civics always bored me to death. She loved all of it. I don't know how many times she made me watch Law and Order, In the Heat of the Night and all that other crap.

Dominique's nigga backed up with his hands held in the air in mock surrender.

"If you ever step to me again, you'll be dead. And bitch, I said what I said already. MY son is doing just fine. Get the fuck out of here."

I sat my gun on my lap and closed the door. Then pulled off, leaving them both standing there. Looking in the rear view mirror I saw the man go over to Domonique getting up in her face toe to toe yelling at her. Yup an insecure abusive nigga like I thought. I wasn't letting BJ around her or him.

I picked up the pastries and some damn hot chocolate for Nya not letting the drama of BJ's biological mother affect any more of my day. I was determined to enjoy the thoughts that kept coming back to me of the time I spent with Drew while he was in town. On the way to the house I made the decision to handle Domonique for good if she stepped to me again and was still on that shit. She would be better off dead, than trying to fuck up her son's life. He was good over here. Shit better than he ever was with her. He was loved and had a good life. Nobody was gonna fuck with my son.

I pulled up to the curb and locked the car doors after grabbing the bag of beignets off the passenger seat. I was trying to lose the extra baby weight since having Joy, but fucking around with Nya's ass, I was gonna stay on the plus size at least until after she had the baby. I went to unlock the front door. But instead of having to put the key in the lock, the door opened before I got the chance.

I screamed out, "Oh my God!" and ran into my brother's arms.

Nya

"Damn, Jolie. You 'bout knocked a nigga over." Saint said after Jolie ran into his arms, excited as hell.

"Stop almost dying, disappearing, and scaring me to death and I won't have to flip the hell out when you come back from the dead nigga. What the hell happened to you anyway?!"

"Don't worry about that."

He brushed her questions off, just like he did when I asked. He was hiding some information from us. Jolie was ecstatic, too damn lit for the morning. But who could blame her. I felt the same way when he first surprised my ass. On top of the other feelings he caused when he first made it back to me.

Just the thought alone had me ready for round 2 this morning. We put the table I was sitting at to good use when we got here after handling my aunt Renae and that other bitch.

I got Saint to admit more about who the other girl was on the way over here. His ass seemed to have amnesia at first, but after I started ignoring him pouting, looking out the window, he fessed up real fucking quick. He couldn't remember her damn name but did tell me that he had fucked her one time. I knew there was more to her being involved just from the way she looked at my nigga back in the club the night of his birthday.

I never forgot a damn thing. My memory was sharp as hell especially when it came to a bitch being all over the man I loved. To this day I still remembered all of the girls Saint messed with when we were teenagers.

Saint came clean about fucking her and about her sister in Houston, running that shit down like none of it mattered to him at all. I believed him because he never gave me a reason not to. Now that he filled me in on the truth shit just felt right. Like all the loose ends were finally being tied up.

The biggest one for me, being my sick ass aunt. Her evil ass deserved more than what I gave her with the bullet to the head. That shit was mercy to be honest. If I was another woman I would have shipped her ass off to be sex trafficked in the black market. I'm sure Saint's family had ties in that shit. But that wasn't me. Plus I was over having my past come back to haunt me.

Now there weren't any more enemies coming for me. As far as Saint, that shit might have been different. I still didn't get the information as to where the fuck he was or who took him. It couldn't have been the two bitches I just took care of. No way did they have enough pull to have him up and disappear. In my bones I felt that it had something to do with his old plug and the other hoe he used to fuck with.

If my nigga didn't fuck these hoes and sling his dick around a lot of problems wouldn't be happening. I stopped myself from thinking that shit though because he had remained faithful to me except the slip up in Houston getting his dick sucked. But even that was when we were just settling into being a couple. Some men were cheaters and others weren't. Saint knew my ass was too damn crazy to play with like that. I already told him once I would end up in jail behind him if some more shit happened moving forward.

We had enough to worry about without more bitches coming in the picture any damn way. I knew this street shit wasn't easy. But most of our entire relationship was spent worrying about who was coming after us. There hadn't been a moment of peace for more than a month or two.

I rubbed my stomach, trying to calm this big ass boy of mine down. Since Saint got home, his ass was wildin' out in here for real cutting up. I was sitting at the head of the dining room table waiting to have the discussion I knew was coming. Saint and Jolie made their way over to the table and pulled up seats on either side of me.

I sat in this spot out of habit. Saint still didn't know the extent that me and Jolie were in control and running shit. He must have had a pretty good ass idea though if Boy said he planned shit to run this way if something happened.

"Start talking. How's shit been goin' while I was gone?" Saint asked looking back and forth between me and Jolie. Her head turning to look at me, just like she always did when it came to business. She deferred to me.

I took a gulp of the water sitting in front of me and then cleared my throat. I don't know why I was so nervous sitting here with the man I loved and my best friend but I was anxious.

"So, me and Jolie been taking care of things like you wanted. Everything's moving good as hell and niggas fell in line real quick on the team. Profits are up and shit is good on the West Bank. Drew…"

"Drew already ran shit down to me 'bout HTown. I'm proud of you two. I knew you would hold shit down and be what the fuck I taught you to be. I appreciate that shit, for real shawty. Jolie." He said serious and sincere at the same time.

Whenever Saint talked business he was straight to the point, no emotion or feelings involved. So for him to say he was proud meant a lot. I was filled with a sense of accomplishment and validation.

"So shit's good over here on the West Bank. What about the rest of the city?" Damn he was smart as hell. He picked up on the fact that I emphasized this part of town when I didn't even realize I had insinuated some shit was up. That was why he was the boss he was.

"Boy just brought some shit to our attention about the downtown crew. Seems like they don't wanna play by the rules no more. We already set up a meeting with uptown for later today. That way we could run the shit by Ron first and make sure he was with it."

"I see. That fuck nigga thought he could change shit up now that my bitch was running shit." He shook his head and clenched his fist talking about Marlo. I noticed all the small details about Saint. Even when he was mad that shit turned me.

"So what you wanna do?" He asked me.

This was him giving me the okay to be involved, however small. Saint could have easily came in here got the rundown and told us he was gonna handle shit. I expected that shit. Especially since I was pregnant about to drop his first son. The way he was over protective of me and Jolie wasn't nothing new.

"You gonna let me help you?" I questioned, with some hope in my voice. I wasn't ready to give this shit up. There was nothing like being the boss and calling the shots. I liked the power, I liked the rush and I damn sure loved the money.

"Slow down, shawty. I mean I can see you been about yo' shit. You and sis. I can respect the hustle. I want your opinion and advice because your smart as hell. I want you by my side and ready to step up to hold shit down whenever necessary. But you gotta understand I can't have you out here moving with me like you been doing while I was away. That shit fucks with me, knowing you were at risk this whole time. You and my seed. What kind of man would I be if I willingly did that shit now? Nah, I'm sorry, but after I hear you out you gotta step back and hold shit down on the home front from here on out."

I listened. I understood, I really did. But I was pissed the fuck off. Who said a woman couldn't do both. A part of me rebelled against the shit Saint was spitting even sitting in silence. I wouldn't argue right now, but I wasn't the type of bitch to take orders and do what I was told. I could handle my own in the streets and at home. Shit, I had been hustling my ass off and busting my ass in the classroom making straight A's along with being the queen behind the operation. Saint even saw how I got down before being with him, taking out Jaquan's ass. No nigga, not even Saint was about to stop me from doing what the fuck I wanted to do.

I nodded my head in understanding and chose to calm myself down before telling him the plans I had. I wanted this shit to smooth over and for the time being I would focus on birthing my son. But when it was said and done, I was determined to not only be by Saint's side for the tough times but really by his side working with him doing the same shit he did all the time. That was how I saw my future. In the streets and in the courtroom as a lawyer. He would see that shit too eventually.

Saint

Nya might have thought I didn't see the look of determination in her eyes when I told her what it was and took the reigns back from her. But I saw that shit. It was the same look I'm sure I got about my organization. She took pride in her work and wanted to stay involved in this shit. But I couldn't put her in it any more than I already had.

I wasn't gonna sit here and be responsible for some shit happening to her when I could stop it. She might not like the shit, but it was what it was. I wasn't the type of nigga to let her run around town doing what the fuck she wanted if it could cost her life.

After she told me her plan to involve Ron and seek out his "help" that only verified the fact she shouldn't be involved. The nigga was solid in the streets for the most part and had looked out holding up his side of our agreement when I came back and took Smoke out. I didn't forget that shit, but at the same time, I knew he had history with Nya. I wasn't feeling the idea of having her ask him for shit. Fuck that.

I was a jealous ass nigga over mine and Nya most definitely was all mine. She was crazy behind me the same way, so we could be crazy together. I wasn't asking for shit again from this nigga especially when the deal benefited him and the downtown crew more than it did our shit over here.

Both locations were on lock now and the territory in Houston and the West Bank were pushing out more product and more dough by the month. The other crews here in New Orleans kept Pedro as their supplier while I was with the competitor. A bigger supplier and bigger fucking cartel. That gave me the upper hand.

When I first switched over I didn't feel the need to breech our agreement changing prices or moving in on their turf. But I could have easily done that shit without too much smoke coming from Downtown or Uptown. At least not enough pressure to fuck up our shit over here. I would rather keep the peace even if it cost me some bread since this was home.

But if either one of them niggas wanted to undercut my team, I could fuck up all their shit. The dope I was getting was purer than the shit Pedro's cartel supplied. I had specifically instructed my lieutenants to whip the shit more than needed, making it lower quality in order to have equal competition. If they didn't want to stick with the terms we set and tried to play me pussy or disrespected my bitch, I would just have my niggas straight drop the shit and fuck up their entire operations.

If my pure shit hit the streets it was over with for them. I could take over the whole damn city. It was that simple and now that I had the New Generation Cartel behind me it would be even easier. Them mothafuckas were all about expansion and making more money from the distribution up here. It was really my call as to how shit played out. Later today I would make the decision based off the feel I got from those niggas. I didn't owe them shit if they weren't keeping their words.

Loyalty was only as good as a mothafuckas word as far as I was concerned. I wasn't saying Ron was with that nigga Marlo on this shit, but it was more likely he knew what the fuck was going on and hadn't brought it to Nya. He might have been in on the shit so she had to come to him and seek out his support. That shit made my blood boil. I never wanted Nya to have to ask another nigga alive for a damn thing other than me. That was my damn job.

I dropped Nya off at home for her to get some rest while I headed out to the meeting. She tried to act like she could fucking do it all and I had to give her credit this street shit even fit her. But shawty was pregnant as fuck. My son would be here any day. She needed to slow her ass down, worry about being a mother and then focus back on her dreams and shit. Not be out here with me.

She wouldn't admit shit, but this dick had her fucked up. Her walk was more labored than it already was with her large stomach. I loved that shit though. Seeing my bitch big, ass fat, titties like some damn watermelons didn't take nothing away from her beauty. I did that shit, and couldn't wait until my son was born.

I damn sure would be a better father than the fuck nigga me and Jolie had and better than our granddaddy. That generational curse shit ended with me. Bet that. I was gonna reinvent the last name "Harris". Only thorough real ass men who held shit down and stood all ten from here on out. My son was my legacy fuck what ya heard.

I was in this shit to win from here on out. That meant in the streets and on the home front. This year had been filled with good shit when it came Nya, but every other fucking thing I would rather just throw away. It was a rough year as far as me taking hits and us taking losses with respect, losing Buck and just straight out being played for pussy by these niggas and bitches that came against me. Martina and Pedro were next on the list. Once they were out of the picture for good, I could sit back and feel like shit was handled.

I leaned back one hand on the steering wheel driving though the hood listening to some old Boosie, headed to the most productive trap I had here. The shit was another shotgun house sitting near the corner where it was easy to run out the back and take off without being caught by the police or niggas trying to rob the shit. There were a few setbacks here, but this bitch was the longest running trap only having to be shut down twice in 3 years.

I walked through the door, past one of my workers standing with an AR around his shoulder. Big Tre was the nigga's name and he was exactly like his name suggested, big as fuck and looked intimidating as hell. I slapped hands with him, speaking first. These niggas were on my team under me but I respected them the same way I expected to get respect back. I wasn't one of those bosses that acted like I couldn't fuck with the help.

I had been in the trap cooking shit for years before me and Buck scored a plug that put us on the map. Big Tre actually reminded me a lot of Buck. Not because Buck was as big even though he was about the same height. But because this nigga never said shit. He never spoke unless it was to Boy, just like Buck didn't say shit to other niggas outside of my ass. They had that same kind of dynamic between them. That shit was solid as hell. The way mothafuckas should be out here. At least having one nigga that had your back and you could count on.

Not having Buck fucked with me on a daily basis. Even though I was grateful to have Drew and he was official, it wasn't like my fucking brother. Buck was the only nigga that would ever be that close to me.

I walked in the room to the kitchen. Big Tre locked the door behind me. This shit wasn't open for business right now. Around noon was the lull of the day, where the least amount of sales happened.

It was when fiends finally found sleep for a little while and the working heads didn't get off work yet. Come around 5:00 this shit would be bumping and pumping out product until the early hours of the next morning. This was the real street life. Day in day out grind, straight hustle the hard way.

I didn't miss the work hours at all but there was benefits to coming from the bottom. If needed I could step in. But I wasn't hands on with none of this shit anymore. I was only out here to show face and talk to Boy before the meeting.

Normally, I didn't come on the block except riding through. I didn't want 12 to have any evidence tying me to this shit. This would be the last time I came through for months at least. Boy was in the kitchen standing next to the stove, getting ready to cook up.

This nigga still cooked the shit himself from the looks of it. I understood that shit, because sometimes mothafuckas couldn't do shit the way you could. The other lieutenants most likely had somebody else cook the shit for them. It was their own call. I was hands off.

Even now, I wasn't gonna intervene with how this nigga ran shit here. I let them all do their own thing unless numbers were fucked up, or some rat shit was going on. By being hands off, I limited my exposure to taking the fall for any of it. I was more of the plug now even though I had a bigger connect I copped shit from.

"Waaah" I greeted him. He was heating up the water in the pot, getting ready to cook the dope.

"Wa's happenin' mane?" he responded.

"How much you got left?"

"252, nigga I'm bout done for the day. Everything good with the shipment?"

I eyed his nigga Big Tre then answered, "Yeah, we're good. After you whip this, I might be changing shit up, straight drop the bitch instead. I'll let you know this afternoon. If that's the case, get the word to the others.

I'm back, and only communicating with you right now, ya heard meh." I told him the plan.

I didn't want to show my face all over, but Boy was solid and stayed true to following my orders about Nya running shit. He enforced that shit from what she told me when some of the other niggas on my own team questioned her. They should have known better, especially when Boy vouched for her. But until there was some all-out disloyalty to me or my bitch then I would let it slide. They would learn to not question shit as long as I had the right mothafuckas' in power.

"That's whats up." He nodded, not asking any more questions.

I walked back out the way I came and hopped in my BMW, headed uptown again. I wasn't looking forward to this sit down. It was probably gonna mean some more fucking bullshit and I was trying to be done with fuck shit. I had bigger plans that I still needed to get accomplished.

I walked into the storefront much like last time, when I came here about that Smoke shit. Normally I would have had Buck sit in on this shit but it was just me. I would have probably had Drew come, but he was in Houston holding shit down running the operation out there right now. He basically

103

lived out there now, only coming back once in a while.

Nothing in the place seemed to change in the few months since I was here. Except the niggas sitting in the game room near the office were nowhere in sight. I was greeted by a nigga at the front desk and one outside of the door to Ron's office but other than that the place was vacant. My senses were alert and the shit seemed off to me. I stayed calm, keeping my hands rested in front of me, clasped by my belt buckle. Still ready to pull my heat if I needed to.

The nigga standing outside the door gave me a head nod and then knocked on the door. Ron came to the shit, opening it wide with a cheesy ass grin on his face. Why the fuck was this nigga smiling so wide seeing my ass? He didn't seem surprised that I was back or anything either. Word probably already got to his ass.

I walked into the office and immediately knew why shit seemed off. The other boss from downtown was already inside sitting down. Marlo was looking real comfortable in one of the chairs at the small round table in the corner of the office. He stood up in greeting and I shook his hand briefly.

The door closed and my guard stayed the fuck up. These two were looking real chummy. All of us had been in a situation

104

where one of us arrived before the others when we met before. But I was getting an entirely different fucking feeling about this shit. They were trying to play me for a fucking bitch.

My mind went back to Nya. What if it had been her and Jolie walking in here to talk to these niggas instead of me? Seems like my ass came back just in time. Who knows how that shit would have went, but I bet my life it would have been some more hoe shit these two niggas would have been on with my bitch and sister.

"Saint, it's good to see you're back." Ron spoke first.

"Oh yeah?... It's good to be back nigga." I answered feeling the tension in every word.

I looked at each of them then let my stare fall on Marlo. "So what's this I hear about your prices?"

Marlo looked out the corner of his eye at Ron, then answered me. "We changed some prices on the hard. You weren't here to discuss the shit. Now your bitch gotta problem with it." He shrugged and I let him get out the rest. I wanted to feel out the entire situation and make sure I had my facts right. "But you're back now, so we can look at our agreement again and see if the shit's beneficial for all of us." He boldly said.

Yeah, this nigga should have kept his mothafuckin' mouth shut like usual. I turned to Ron and let him get his two cents in, with my eyebrows raised waiting for his input.

"It's true NyAsia held shit down while you were gone, but this shit was with us not her. I looked at the numbers and everything checks out. We can all make more money on this shit." Ron finished like the shit he said made the most fucking sense in the world.

Both of them just fucked up and didn't even know how bad. Not only did they breech their agreement trying to change shit up while I was gone stepping on my damn toes. They tried to take advantage of the fact Nya was running things for me. Calling the shots without the agreement from the West Bank. That was some real bitch ass shit. And the way this nigga Marlo spoke on Nya made me wanna kill his ass, along with the fuck nigga Ron using her full name in my presence. I understood they knew each other as kids, but everyone called her Nya. This nigga just sat right in my fucking face trying to be disrespectful acting like they had more history than they did.

I chose to end this shit. Just that abruptly I stood up, adjusted my shirt and walked the fuck out. I wasn't gonna discuss shit with these disloyal ass niggas. They came against me. I didn't need to go to go back and forth with these mothafuckas, go to war, talk shit, none of that. I already won and they didn't know it yet. Numbers wouldn't fucking lie just like Ron suggested. But mine were incomparable. That pure shit was about to flood the mothafuckin' streets tomorrow.

New Orleans was mine.

Drew

I stood out front, knocked on the door one time and was happy as fuck when Jolie swung the shit open with a smile on her face. Damn she was beautiful as hell and she was mine now. I never wanted to be thankful that my homeboy was taken out, but I was thankful to be the man that could be here for her now.

I wasn't spiritual and didn't even know if God was real, but I did live with the mentality that there was no second guessing shit. What we had felt right and I really believed Buck would have wanted Jolie to be happy and looked out for, rather than go at this shit alone.

She was more than just a fuck for me. When I first told her that I had feelings for her that was more than I could say about any other woman besides my mother. That said a lot. I was an only child on my mother's side. As far as my pops went, I didn't have a clue where the fuck his ass was at. All I had to go by was his name but I never tried to find the mothafucka.

My mother was the mom and the dad growing up and she was my very first queen. Jolie was the only woman that was worth treating the same way. There was just something about her smile and dimples that first got me hooked, even with the tears and sadness at the time. I saw the light in her. That corny shit got me chasing behind her ass from the first time she called me just to talk, as she used to say when she was depressed in the hotel room alone after Buck was shot down.

Jolie untied her robe still in the doorway, giving me a nice view of her fat bare pussy. I slid my hand around her waist and pushed her back into the living room past the entry until her thighs were against the back of the couch. She stood still looking up at me with those eyes, that let me know lil' baby was ready for the dick. The same way I was ready for the pussy.

Since I stayed in Houston most of the time and she was still living here, whenever I was in town or she came to see me all we did was chill out and have sex now that we were in a relationship. I wasn't complaining about the shit. But I didn't want her to think this shit was just a booty call. I wanted our relationship to work for the long haul.

She lowered her gaze letting her eyes trace over my chest and torso, tracing her hand over my abs. Then reaching lower into my waistband placing her cold hand on my dick. Her hand instantly warmed up from the contact. Keeping her grip she slid her hand back and forth. I didn't need any help getting ready. The minute I saw her, even before the robe fell open, my dick was rock hard.

Jolie brought her hand back out and then undid my pants. I reached for my piece and placed it down on the couch behind her. Then stood still staring down, letting her do her thing.

"Drew, I missed you."

"Oh yeah?"

"Yes, baby, I been waiting for you all day."

"Tell me about that shit." I told her leading her on.

"... Well, when I woke up, my pussy was wet thinking about your big dick. I thought about you filling me up and fucking me. All day, my mind kept coming back to you. So I touched myself and imagined it was you inside me. Your body, strong arms and your mouth all over me." She kept going, talking that nasty shit to me, knowing she had me in the palm of her hand.

Her hands roaming around, easing off each item of clothing I had on in the process of her talking slow and seductive. Kissing my chest, sucking on different parts of my neck as she stood on her tiptoes.

I kept my hands to myself so far but when her tongue found my mouth I lost control and gripped her ass, lifting her up. Placing her ass on the back of the couch

111

going to fucking work. Then exchanged touches and kisses making my way down to her pussy. I kneeled down, my hands squeezing behind her knees spreading her legs wide. Tonguing the fuck out of my bitch's pussy.

Jolie was always clean as hell and smelled like fruit. Her juices tasted like that shit too. I flicked my tongue over her clit and worked one of my hands around her pussy finding her tight entrance. When I stuck the first finger in, I looked up kissing her inner thigh watching her body respond to my touch.

I began working my hand faster adding another finger stretching her like she wanted. That shit had her going wild riding my hand like it was my dick. She threw her head back body shaking, pussy locked the fuck down on my fingers making it hard to move them.

Damn. Her shit was tight as fuck. I kept up the same rhythm and dug in deeper. Her eyes were closed, body bucking hard. I replaced my fingers with my tongue at the last minute. Switching shit up sucking on her clit hard sticking one finger in her ass.

She tensed up before her cum flowed into my mouth and down my chin. Jolie held onto the back of my head continuing to ride my fucking face with me getting every drop. I let her finish getting herself together.

Then I stood back up and turned her around, gripping the fuck out of her fat ass again. Jolie's ass was some real life donk shit. She had this tiny ass waist that I could hold onto while watching this bitch bounce back like some movie shit. I loved all of her body, the thickness, the dimples and stretch marks. It was all her and sexy as fuck.

I eased my dick in her inch by inch, until most of me was in and my shit was touching the base of her pussy. All the bitches lost their minds behind my dick, talking about it wasn't regular "white boy" shit, but the fuck if I knew what was normal. I was just blessed to be able to please women and was happy to help when they needed some dick.

Now this shit was exclusive and all Jolie's. So far she had handled the mothafucka just fine even though she complained about me fucking up her insides.

I let her get adjusted and gave her time to start her own rhythm bouncing back on my dick working her pussy on me.

"Damn, why are you so big? Fuck, you feel good." Jolie said quietly, between the light strokes.

Fuck that, I wanted to hear that shit. I started working with her moving my hips into her as she threw the shit back, causing her to lean completely over the back of the couch.

Making that ass come up in the air more. I started really working her ass out and throwing the dick on her. Her pussy tightened up the same way it had on my hand.

I reached forward and gripped her titties from underneath, applying pressure to her nipples at the same time she cummed, screaming out the way I wanted,

"Fuck, Drew, damn!"

"That's right, say that shit. Don't hold it in." I added.

"Why you do me like that bae? You know I was putting it on your ass." She joked getting herself partly composed.

My dick was still hard as fuck inside her but I kept moving nice and slow waiting for her. Jolie was one of the only bitches I ever fucked that could keep going and cum back to back. Most hoes only busted once and then their shit dried up, but her pussy was like a faucet.

"Jolie, you better take this dick, like I taught you." I said serious as hell, letting her know I wasn't done with her yet. I was only busting after I made her cum a few times.

Then she started twerking on my dick trying to prove a point. I loved the shit, I loved the way she fucked me. The way her pussy fit my dick. I loved this damn girl.

I was caught up thinking and didn't realized how hard I had started going. But Jolie was keeping up with my ass still throwing her pussy back hard against my pelvis with the deep strokes. I wrapped my hands around her waist, feeling her pussy from the front. Finding her clit with my fingers and cupping her mound, still stroking her. I slowed down watching her ass bounce each time I came forward.

"Drew!" She got louder than before, sounding like she needed something.

I knew what the fuck that meant. She was about to rain down on my dick again. So I lowered both my hands, holding firmly onto her shoulders, digging her out with her feet coming up off the floor.

"That's right, take it all."

I let her have all the dick back to back. Her pussy squeezing down trying to lock me in place. Still pushing through the friction until she exploded and her pussy squirted out. Now the room was filled with moans and the slapping noise from how wet she was. I moved in circular motions as my dick jerked and cum shot out. This shit felt so damn good.

Jolie screamed out my name again. "DREW!!!!" It was pain, pleasure and anger all at one.

Fuck, I fucked up. I was supposed to pull out. But the shit felt too fucking good. Her pussy fucked up my head.

Nya

Since having the meeting a few weeks
ago, Saint had been doing every damn thing
in his power to keep me out of the streets.
His ass was so stubborn, every time I brought
the subject up and tried to get some kind of
information form him he started taking off my
clothes, kissing on my neck, or talking about
our son. Any and everything he could to
distract me. But his ass wasn't slick. I knew
what he was doing. So far I just let him get
his way because I was partly still in shock
that he was actually back and I really did
need to rest.

My ass had put in so much damn work
for the last 6 months going nonstop day in
day out. But now that he was here I was
enjoying the break. Even though I was still in
college, my fall semester just wrapped up last
week and now I was taking a break form that
also. Until the summer semester when I
would be right back at them books working
towards my degree. School was like a drug to
me, I couldn't get enough of my education.

I was glad Terrell was all about his shit
too. Soon he would be joining me in the
college life. It was unbelievable in a way since
I had raised him and now we would be at a
similar stage in life. But I wouldn't have the
shit any other way. If our parents were still

here they would have expected us to do nothing but take our asses to school anyway. It was always an expectation in our household. I remember them talking to us at an early age about school and the importance of making something of ourselves, to be better than them.

But in my eyes they were damn near perfect. I appreciated their hard work and the quiet lifestyle they lived. Even Jolie used to love coming over and would always talk about how "dope" my parents were. This was the shit I tried to remember instead of the bullshit that happened after they were gone.

Now that I was about to be somebody's mother I wondered what my parents would say. How it would be to have them here as grandparents and if they would approve of Saint. They sort of knew Saint, but only as Jolie's brother. My momma and daddy never asked much about their parents or anything else about either of them. Even though my parents stayed to themselves they still knew who everybody's family was. That was just how shit was in the hood, everybody knew everybody back a few generations.

I was sure Saint would have charmed his way into at least my mother's heart. Now my daddy never played about me even having a boyfriend. He was strict as hell about dating when I was 15, the last time I saw him.

I took a deep breath, thinking about them and looking in the mirror of the dressing table I had purchased. I added this piece to the room decor Saint had. Last night I hadn't got hardly any sleep. I was just too big, ready to have Kwamir like 2 days ago, when it was my real due date. Thankfully the doctor agreed to induce me by Monday if he didn't come yet. Today was Friday, so the reality of it all was starting to set in. Come next week, I was gonna be a mother. This shit was real.

Saint left early this morning, heading out like usual and only telling me he was going to the restaurant for the day. Mmmhhhmmm, my ass I thought. He was keeping me in the dark about what he was really doing. This nigga must have forgot I wasn't dumb.

I finished throwing my fresh braids into a high bun on top of my head and putting on some gold hoop earrings. All I wore these days were sun dresses with slides even though the weather was turning cold as hell being that it was December. Shit, when I went outside I at least added a sweater. That was good enough. I know I wasn't looking my best but at least my face and hair were on point. Right now all I cared about was comfort. And Saint said he loved the way I looked. His ass couldn't get enough of me no matter what I was wearing. The shit was usually coming off anyway.

It was the only thing comfortable, if I couldn't be naked. And believe me most the time these last couple of weeks when I was alone in the house during the day, my ass was naked. Whether because of Saint or because I just was more comfortable than with fabric against any part of my sensitive skin. Some days all I put on was a robe here lately.

Today I was on my way to the bookstore and running some other errands before meeting up with Jolie and Saint later for dinner. I had an urge to get up and go out, handling some of the shit I had been putting off. It was all things I wanted to take care of before the baby came.

I walked over to the front door and pushed the remote starter for my Benz so it would be warm when I got in. It looked cold outside, well cold enough for a bitch like me from the south. I went in the kitchen grabbed my thermos of coffee that I already fixed and sat up on one of the stools at the counter for a few minutes waiting for the car.

I scrolled through Instagram seeing what was popping on the Shadroom this morning and all the other celebrity news. I remembered not even having a real cell phone with data and shit only a year ago. A year was such a short time for shit to change up so drastically. Every day I woke up grateful and ready to tackle the day ahead. It was true that a person could get a whole new outlook on life because that shit happened to me.

Standing up was even getting harder these days. I walked slowly to the door, making my way out to my car. Then slid into the leather seat enjoying the warmth from the heated seats on my back and ass. Taking a minute to catch my breath, I inspected my light makeup and added some rose colored lip gloss that contrasted against my dark skin.

Then put the car in reverse and headed out to the bank down the street first. After going through the drive through, I drove across the bridge to downtown. I planned to stop by the bookstore and then the nail salon. I wanted to get my nails off before Kwamir was here.

I still wasn't all the way used to this high maintenance shit the life I was living called for. I was under pressure of wearing only the best shit, having my hair slayed and always being and having the best of the best. That was what others expected to see knowing I was Saint's bitch.

Saint never told me to wear certain things or cared what the fuck I had on for that matter. But it was a respect thing for me. If my nigga was the head of a big time drug operation and a successful business man then I knew I was a representation of him. He spoiled me with gifts, diamonds, all the things a woman like me loved. But sometimes it was a fucking lot to deal with.

I swear I loved Saint and wanted to hold him down making sure he wasn't embarrassed to have me on his arm. Even when he was away I kept this shit up, but it just wasn't me. I could just as easily go without any of this extra shit and be perfectly content.

Some of the bomb ass clothes and jewelry were nice though and I did appreciate everything. The everyday part was what was hard for me. That was the benefit of being pregnant because I could get away with more shit without people judging me. One of my insecurities was that I never felt good enough for Saint.

I knew Saint loved me with or without doing a damn thing, just like now with my off the damn wall outfits he had seen me in the last couple of weeks. I couldn't stop thinking about my man no matter what I was doing, damn.

I walked to the bookstore on the opposite side from where I parked on the curb. Seeing my reflection in the glass storefront gave me a little more confidence in my looks. I was still pulling off my outfit. At least everything I had on matched from the long maroon knit dress, that clung to my curves to the black slides and socks. It was actually kind of working for me. Fuck what everybody thought today.

I mean I looked pregnant. Shit, my ass was beyond pregnant. Luckily this boy was all in my stomach and I wasn't spreading out the way they said girls had you. He was giving me more ass and titties, while everywhere else was still on point.

I opened the glass door and went straight to the nonfiction section in the store. Finding about five books all on SAT and ACT prep. Normally, Terrell would have already taken his tests last year, but everything was a little delayed due to all the turmoil. So now he had to rush and take both tests right after Christmas break, then hurry up and apply for colleges as soon as he got his results back. I had faith that my brother would get high scores. His ass was smart as hell. I just wanted to make sure he was as prepared as possible.

As I was walking back to my Benz, another familiar car rolled up and parked behind me. It was Ron's black Benz, an older version of the same kind as mine. My guard went up immediately. It was no coincidence that this nigga just so happened to be riding through and stop right behind me. Even if he did this shit because he spotted me it was still suspect.

I still didn't know how shit went with the meeting Saint had with him or the downtown boss that I originally set up. Maybe that was what set off the red flags. Ron was always cool as hell and we had been friends, kind of, as kids. So I shouldn't be worried about why he was parking next to me.

He got out of his car and walked over to where I was standing on the sidewalk. I decided to wait and speak before getting back in my car. When he came up to me he had a strange ass look on his face then replaced it with a different one. He raked his eyes up and down my very pregnant body and I swear to God licked his lips.

I had been around this nigga only a handful of times during the time when Saint was gone, but never once did his ass give me a look the way he was now. Otherwise my ass would have never been near him. He was making me feel real uncomfortable. I knew niggas well enough to know when their intentions weren't pure. And this nigga was up to some shit.

I backed up. He must have noticed my disinterest and tried to play shit off.

"Wassup NyAsia..." He said like he was coming on to me. Yeah real out of pocket disrespectful.

"Hey Ron. Nothing much. Just out getting some books." I kept it short and simple.

"Damn, Your nigga can't take care of that for you?... I mean you 'bout to have yo' baby and shit, I'm just saying." He said, trying to recover when he noticed my look of disapproval.

I scrunched up my face with my eyebrows raised and gave this nigga the look of death. No way was he gonna stand in my face and disrespect my man, the father of my baby. And his ass should know better anyway. I was never into him even back in the day like he was into me. I always loved Saint. From day fucking one. Maybe that was why he was so damn salty about the shit. In my eyes he was never more than a family friend.

I shrugged the whole encounter off and walked over to the driver side door of my car, opening it up.

"We might have known each other since we were kids, but don't get shit twisted

Ron. Saint is MY nigga and always will be. Don't disrespect him, or play yourself out here." I responded and got in my car.

It was a real shame I had to come off as a bitch and probably fuck up our kind of friendship. But his ass should have never in his life came for what was mine. I would still cut a nigga real quick. He didn't know a damn thing about me that was for sure.

I turned the music up and finished my morning with a quick visit to the nail salon that only took 15 minutes. By the time my nails were off I was tired as hell and having some back pains. This extra weight was really fucking with me and making me go crazy. I kept trying to remind myself that it was all worth it.

I heard my phone buzzing and reached inside my handbag to see Saint's name pop up. I answered it right away, smiling ear to ear. Damn I loved my man.

"What that nigga want?" He asked catching me off guard.

I already knew who he was talking about, but didn't know how he knew. I didn't question him. His tone let me know that he was ready to murder Ron. I wasn't trying to have him take out his bad ass temper on me when I didn't do shit wrong this time.

"Nothing. He tried to say some slick shit and I shut his ass down, that's all."

"That's all?!" He said incredulously, like he thought I was trying to downplay shit.

I knew Ron was on bullshit, but I didn't want to be the cause of more drama in our lives.

"You know I can handle myself. I'm good. He knows better than try some shit. I'm on my way to the restaurant now, *daddy*. I wanted to see about you." I switched the subject up. The same way he had been doing me whenever I wanted more information about the streets lately.

"Nya, that shit ain't gonna work. But you're right, bring that ass hear NOW." His deep voice sent vibrations through my body down to my pussy. Making the bitch leak already.

"Bet" I ended the call.

I knew he hated when I did that shit, ending the call like I was the man in this relationship. But I wanted him to put me in my place. I loved that side to him just as much as I loved the sweet loving side. My nigga was the gangsta version Dr. Jeckel and Mr. Hyde and I was the only one who could tame him. All bets were off when we went at it.

I pulled up to his restaurant parking lot damn near racing, trying to get to him. Since it was early afternoon the restaurant was still closed with the workers preparing to

127

open for the evening. I walked my happy ass right inside trying not to smile from the anticipation of seeing Saint. Like I didn't wake up to him giving me a juicy kiss before he left our house this morning. I would never get enough of Kwame "Saint" Harris.

I figured he was in his office, so I entered in through the kitchen and walked towards it, not paying none of the workers any mind. They were used to seeing my ass anyway. I had to come and check on things from time to time when Saint was locked up in Mexico. Yes his ass finally told me where he really was all his time.

Saint appeared at t the end of the short hallway that led to his office. Standing with his legs in a straight dominant stance. Wearing a pair of distressed baggy jeans sagged slightly, a black shirt that had a white SUPER logo on the front, and a fitted hat. My nigga looked like a certified gangsta straight off the block. I loved that shit about Saint. It was a whole hell of lot easier for a man to look good without the extra effort.

To look at him and not know who he was, you wouldn't think he was the owner of not one but multiple successful business. He was all the way grown and sexy in a street way. He did dress it up and put on some fancy shit when necessary, but on the regular he was just an everyday type of nigga. The same way I was just an everyday type bitch. With a lot of fucking commas in both our bank accounts.

He turned his head when he caught one of the young ass cooks looking at me and cut his eyes real quick shutting that shit down. I hadn't even noticed that shit. My eyes were trained on only one man.

Saint moved his hands to his front and clasped them together right below his waistband. Of course my eyes went down too. I already knew that his dick was hard. I looked back up giving him that knowing look with a smirk. I had his ass. When I came closer to him he gave me a deep kiss, then moved to the side after we broke apart so I could walk in the office ahead of him.

It was little shit like him having me lead in front with him in the back. Shit like that, where he acted as my protector that made me feel safe and secure. Even the strongest woman appreciated a strong ass man to have her back. We needed that shit.

He surprised me with reaching out and palming my ass with both hands while I took the final few steps to the office door.

"Your ass is fat as fuck. I'm bout to make that bitch bigger." He was so damn stupid.

I laughed him off and opened the door. He let it close behind him and then came up behind me wrapping his arms around my waist from behind, walking me slowly but pointedly over to his desk.

Dick pressed against the crack of my ass and the heat between us already building. Then Saint abruptly stopped pressed my back down. I braced myself with my hands on his desk. I knew exactly what time it was.

"Give me the dick bae." I tried saying sweetly, knowing this wasn't that kind of sex.

"You know it ain't that." He answered reading my mind. Yeah I knew and my pussy dripped thinking about it.

"You think that shit's cute? You can handle yourself and all that bullshit?!" He asked but I knew he didn't want answers yet.

He yanked my dress up and pushed it up to my middle back, letting my bare ass sit in his face, while I was bent over like a pretzel.

"Damn shawty, it's like that." He slid one of his fingers in without touching any other part of my body. My walls tightened, juices coating his finger. I was already leaking. He had my ass.

"Mmmhhhmm, just like that." I moaned

Saint moved his hand out and I instantly missed it. But he quickly changed shit up, pinching my clit clasping it with his hand. My nipples hardened. My already sensitive skin was electrified, like a thousand bolts of electricity shooting all over from my pussy.

He rolled his fingers and thumb back and forth over it. Then let go again. What the hell was this nigga doing to me? I kept my eyes trained straight ahead waiting for more, body trembling from the pain and pleasure.

I heard his pants drop to the floor and got ready for what I knew was coming. Already clinging to the edge of the desk waiting for him to fill me up. Knowing what was coming didn't stop the effect of Saint penetrating me.

He slid in deep and hard slamming his entire dick into the base of my pussy. He fucked up my entire world with the full force of his dick. His hands on the front of my thighs, keeping me right the fuck in place. Whenever we fucked it was passionate and we both got caught up in the feelings. Even now, pregnant as hell the sex was off the damn chain.

I knew if I wasn't so dark, I would have bruises from how he was handling me, but everything felt so damn good.

"Wait, Saint, Damn" I hissed out, trying to recover from him all but tearing me in two.

"Nah, baby since you can handle yourself, show your nigga. All that talk and no show?!" He challenged. It was on now.

I sucked that shit up and soon the pain was replaced by nothing but pleasure. I pressed my pussy back into him with every stroke. Matching him, handling myself like he wanted me to. Slapping noises and moans echoed throughout the otherwise empty room. Saint's dick got harder like he was about to cum.

Instead this mothafucka pulled out and turned me around. Kissing me on the side of the neck, the only sign of being gentle. He lifted me up, sitting me down on the edge of the desk like it was nothing. I pulled the dress completely off over my head. Then wrapped my hands around Saint's neck. He used his hands to spread my legs wide holding onto my knees.

My pussy was soaking wet, waiting for him to fuck me more. Growing impatient, I let go of his neck with one hand and gripped his dick, bringing it to my pussy. Instead of sliding all the way in, Saint stopped part way after I let go. Using only the tip of his dick to fuck me. I loved when he did this shit, working the head of his dick in and out my pussy.

I leaned back further letting go of his neck bracing myself on my elbows, causing

132

my pussy to come up at an angle. Saint's dick going deeper with each stroke. Sliding in and out rubbing against my clit forcing my hips to move with him.

This nigga switched his grip bringing his hands down to my ass. My pussy tightened up even more with him all the way planted deep inside me. I wrapped my legs around him still leaning back rubbing on my breasts. Really starting to fuck him back picking up the pace myself. Pregnant or not, I was hanging in there with him just fine, putting this damn pussy on his ass too.

"I can handle... the dick... just fine!!" I screamed out, head thrown back. Fuck who heard.

But as soon as I said that shit, I was fucked up again. He was just so damn big. He pushed himself deeper and rotated his hips side to side hitting every damn wall I had, putting more pressure on my cervix. Every part of me was tense, hard and soaking wet.

"Take the mothafucka then." He grunted out and then pushed into me one final time as he busted deep in me, my cum gushing all over his dick.

I laid all the way back on his desk for a second to get myself together, letting my breathing slow back down. Saint squeezed my ass, coming forward first kissing me on the lips then placing a light kiss on my round stomach. He slid his dick out of and helped me to sit up.

I sat there starting up at Saint. His light brown chest glistening from the work he put in and his dick shiny wet with my juices all over him. He was the best. The best everything. I took his presence in in and enjoyed all of him for a moment. I was at complete peace. Everything was finally right.

Saint

I followed Nya into the bathroom attached to my office and sat her ass right up on the marble counter. Then spread her legs, took the wash rag from her hands and ran the warm water through it in the sink. Her stomach protruded in my face, and I placed another kiss on that bitch. Right here in this mothafuckin' bathroom was the shit that really mattered. It was small things like being able to wash my bitch and simply be here with her that made a nigga like me feel like this street shit was worth it. It was worth more than all the money in the fucking world.

"Really daddy? You trying some shit now." Nya spoke up.

I noticed the chill bumps all over her thighs and stomach. Damn, I actually wasn't trying to start some shit. But she had the prettiest fucking pussy, I couldn't help the shit. I put another soft kiss on her fat waxed pussy. When we first got together she just shaved, now she made appointments to get waxed. It was a whole lot of shit that upgraded in her life since getting with me.

I was good with however Nya took care of herself. She was clean as hell and I would still eat the fuck out of that pussy. She tasted good as fuck and I loved to make her bust, seeing that shit up close and personal. But her extra effort didn't go unnoticed either. Real shit, a partner should upgrade your life. That was the same way she did me.

A lot of mothafuckas probably looked at me as a nigga who had it all before I got with Nya. But the truth was she made me want to be a better man every day. After being locked up in fucking Mexcio for 6 months, my head was on fucking straight and my mind was clear. Nya was about to be my damn wife.

I was working on surprising her ass. But wanted to wait until the birth of our son and shit settled down first. But not wait that damn long. There was too much uncertainty in this life.

"Nah, baby that pussy trying some shit talking to me. But I'm gonna be talking to her later, ya heard meh." I stood up and slapped her thigh, before helping her off the counter.

Damn she was sexy as hell and if we had more time, I damn sure would be taking care of her again. No matter how much I got it was never enough. I was a sexual ass nigga. Before Nya, not a single bitch could even handle this dick, now she owned the mothafucka. So yeah her ass was 'bout to be officially locked down. Last name and all. I was serious about changing my family name for generations and Nya was at the center of my ambition.

"You better keep your promise Saint." Nya leaned in for a kiss.

Our lips met. Anticipation was a mothafucka. I followed her out of the bathroom. Then fixed my clothes in the full length mirror on the back of the closet door. I had this office custom designed after I bought the building from another restaurant that failed. I needed to have shit a certain way for the life I lived.

In the closet were several different clothes from a suit to some all black combat shit. There was a false back that opened up to a state of the art safe filled with gold, a few bands in bills and 2 semi's. I added the gold after the shit with Smoke. I needed to always plan for the worst and hope for the best.

Thinking ahead left this operation in New Orleans running like a fucking machine while I was gone. Boy knew that Jolie and Nya were supposed to step up in my absence without any fucking questions. I wasn't gonna have a team that questioned my choices even when I wasn't on scene. The only two people I fully trusted were bitches and the niggas up under me had to deal with that shit forever. Even though I trusted Drew to some extent, he wasn't family.

It was around 3:00. The place didn't open unit 4. But Jolie wanted to meet up and talk over a late lunch, so I set it up for the staff to do their thing for us before opening for the day. That way she could say what she wanted to say without distractions. My sister loved to fucking talk, so there was no telling what was on her mind or would come out of her mouth. Don't get me wrong I loved her fucking life and we were close as hell, but she aggravated me to death sometimes like most sisters.

Nya went and sat at our usual table in the corner of the restaurant, sitting all the way in the back against the far wall. It was the best table. A booth that gave you a view of the entire floor. She had to sit on the edge these days to accommodate her big ass stomach.

I had unintentionally made a joke of that shit the first time she had to do it last week when we ate dinner here. She made my ass pay for it. She sat silent through the rest of dinner. Then at home she let me eat her pussy, but refused to let me fuck. Until I just said "fuck it" and we fell asleep. Of course I didn't let her get off that easy. I slid up in those guts while her ass was still asleep. Waking her up to my dick making her cum. And all was forgiven. This pregnancy shit had her feelings all fucked up.

Jolie came in after the waitress brought over our waters looking happy as hell. That shit was refreshing to see. When all that shit

138

went down with those pussy niggas taking Nya and me ending up in Mexico locked up, she was still trying to piece back together her life. My sister was always a person to bounce back, nothing could keep her down. But she loved my nigga and her having his baby couldn't be easy for her. I wanted to protect my little sister. But the shit she went through losing Buck was something I couldn't shield her from.

Her having my niece still tripped me out sometimes. Joy was a small version of Buck and Jolie mixed together. She had some of Bucks features but had my sister's beauty. Without my partna here, I was gonna be the father figure in her life. She would be taken care of and that was on God.

After Jolie sat down at the table, Drew came through the front door following behind my employee who first unlocked it for Jolie did the shit again. I wasn't expecting another person to be coming through the doors until we opened for the day. Now I knew what this shit was about. But I would sit back and see if I was right.

Drew was still bouncing back and forth between staying here and Houston. Sooner or later, his ass was just gonna have to find a spot permanently and make a decision. But he would figure that shit out himself. As long as business was good, then whatever the fuck he did on his own time was on him.

Drew wasn't the type who flaunted his personal business in the streets. Even the bitches he fucked with knew their place and didn't come out of pocket much. Shit we all had some fucking headaches to deal with. He had one bitch just about stalking him when he first came to town a few years back before I planted him out in Houston. I saw that girl one time on some ratchet shit trying to catch my man up for talking to another hoe at a block party.

He was all hugged up with the girl and his ex came up behind him. She started bum rushing him, slapping the shit out of his neck and back. Then turned to punches. I had to give it to him, he kept his composure as pissed off as he was and turned around unfazed. Grabbed her by the wrists and then gave her a big ass bear hug, picking her ass up. Drew walked her right the fuck over to his ride and sat her ass down in the backseat. He was cold with the shit, didn't even let the bitch ride shotgun.

Me, Buck and the rest of the niggas standing around got a kick out of that shit. Drew even came back and gamed the other bitch still standing right where he left her. You would have thought the shit would have sent her on her way running for the hills. But not the type of bitches Drew went for. They were straight hoodrats, real gutta bitches. She smiled and leaned in making a bigger fucking scene giving him a sloppy ass kiss and pressing her body against his. That shit had the whole block rolling.

He slapped the girl on the ass and went back to his car, driving off handling his shit like a real G. Needless to say that bitch never came around us again. Matter of fact, every time I spotted her at some shit and Drew was there she turned the fuck around and did a U turn. The way he handled shit was initially what made me think he could handle bigger shit in the streets.

He wasn't with that flashy shit and was smart enough to keep the drama the fuck away from the team. That shit was hard to come by. Plus the way he dealt with everything in Houston. I didn't know another mothafucka alive that could get some shit like that done with little to no problems.

Drew came over to the booth and instead of just greeting me with a head nod and having me step away for a quick minute to see what the hell was up, this man sat the down. Sitting real fucking close to my sister, letting his arm fall across her shoulders. It was a good thing I already knew what the hell was up.

I turned and looked at Nya. She seemed surprised. So I turned back towards my sister.

"Me and Drew are seeing each other. We've been talking for a minute and now... things are more serious. I wanted to do shit right this time and not keep it in the dark from you." Her eyes met mine. "He treats me good, he's here for me and someone I trust. I want you to accept us being a couple and give your blessing." She pleaded her case.

But she didn't need to do that shit. Whether I approved or not of whatever the fuck they had going on, my sister was able to make her own decisions. Her feeling like she had to come to me and get my approval felt like I really let her the fuck down with how I reacted to shit last time. "Last time". Yeah, the shit rubbed me the wrong way. It was not only awkward as hell to think about Drew with my sister, but also for her to get with another person on my team. She didn't know I already gave my blessing to Drew though. She was the one in for a damn surprise.

"It's your life. This shit's on you. But I ain't gonna sit here and sugar coat shit. You really wanna go this route? Being with him means the same shit could happen to him that you already went through with Buck. You want that kind of life?" I asked.

Her relationship was her business, but I wanted her to go into this shit eyes wide open, not believing in that fairy tale shit. She knew I was a realistic ass nigga. This life wasn't what most people thought. Yeah we had ends for fucking days, but all that shit came with a cost. Safety and security was the price we all paid. Nya was built for this shit and the kids would be protected at all costs. But there was still no telling on the day to day.

Jolie was a fucking school teacher. She was optimistic and always chasing some kind of fairy tale life. The marriage, stable home, shit she missed out on from her own damn parents.

"I'm good. I know what it is to love a man in the streets. Shit, that's all I know. From you, to Buck, and now being with Drew." She changed her line of sight and put it on Drew briefly.

I caught that shit. She was in love with his ass and I bet anything he was in love with her ass from how he was acting. This shit must have been more serious than I initially thought.

I ended the conversation by nodding my head and motioning for the waitress to come back over. She took their drink orders and then brought out the bread appetizers. This shit was good as fuck served with a cheese dipping sauce or butter option. The restaurant proceeded to open at 4 like usual, with a few early older couples coming through the doors shortly after. We got our food and were comfortably eating off our plates.

My restaurant served all the good shit from seafood to basic shit like chicken and waffles, gumbo, all the shit people from the south liked to eat. I wasn't biased just because I owned the place either, this bitch got five star reviews from tourists and locals alike. Now I didn't know if that shit would have happened if the mothafuckas knew the owner was flooding these damn streets with narcotics and my dirty money was funneling in here. But fuck it. What they didn't know didn't hurt shit.

"I want to stop by Joe's to get some doughnuts on the way home" Nya's greedy ass said.

"We got dessert right here shawty. That shit don't make no damn sense." I half teased.

She already knew she was getting her fucking way.

"Whatever, your restaurant good and all, but does it have doughnuts?! No, the fuck it doesn't. Don't try that slick shit with me Saint. You know it's all your damn fault anyway. Your son wants what he wants. Next time pull out nigga." Her mouth was lethal.

Nya never held shit back. Sometimes she would sit back and listen when it was serious. Then she was more reserved. But when it came to me or family she said what she said. I knew her ass was trying to be funny but that shit was too much, talking 'bout pull out. She knew better than that shit. Drew and Jolie thought the shit was funny as hell.

I cut my eyes at Nya and placed my hand on her thick thigh, pressing down tight enough. All that did was make her spoiled ass smile. I already promised to eat her pussy for dessert, so some damn doughnuts was the last fucking thing on my mind. Her reckless mouth turned me the fuck on more and made me want to take her to my office again.

My eyes switched over quick as hell, watching some bum ass nigga walking over to our table. Before he made it all the way, Drew turned around to see what caught my attention and stood up himself at about the same time I did. My hand went to my back the same way his went to the front where we kept our tools.

I didn't know this nigga. Never seen him around here and anybody from this fucking area I had seen before. He had some shit with him, to be trying to approach me in my fucking restaurant like this. With my family here. Whatever he was coming over to our table for he would be better off turning the fuck back around. I already knew what type of nigga he was from the look on his face and the way he carried himself.

The clothes he was wearing looked brand new, but they didn't fit him. He was fucking counterfeit to the fucking bone. When you're in the streets your whole life you know when shit fits and he was either a rat or a bitch. Or both. But his ass was grimy either way. I already had my guard up with the shit with Pedro still not being all the way settled. But my gut told me this didn't have shit to do with him or Martina's ass.

He took the final steps over and stopped in front of Drew, hands going straight to his pockets. The nigga had braids going back, was light skinned and about the same height as Drew, shorter than me. He wore a fake ass gaudy gold chain to top the shit off.

"Waaahh" He tried to greet us like his ass was from around here. Strike fucking one. He sounded so fucking retarded that it was hard not to laugh at this clown ass nigga. But the nerve of him to approach me not having ever met me, made me take this shit serious. You always had to watch out for niggas like him. It was this type to be waiting in the cut to fuck some shit up.

Me and Drew stood in silence, still waiting.

To us this was already a standoff, daring him to do some shit. A restaurant with witnesses wasn't gonna stop me from protecting my sister or Nya. A life sentence or a fucking death sentence wasn't stopping shit behind those two.

"I wanted to come and introduce myself since I'm gonna be around now. I know how that respect shit goes and didn't wanna step on any toes." He looked past Drew to me.

I gave him a blank stare back, letting him continue. Then he fucked up again, looking down in Jolie's face then back to me. I watched intently feeling shit out.

"Ask her. She knows who I am. I'm BJ's step father now. I know he ain't been coming 'round his mother and I want that shit to change. I figured coming to you man to man, being that you got a baby on the way, you would understand how important family is."

"Fuck you say?" I said calmly and got in the nigga's face staring him the fuck down. Tension was high. Before his pussy ass could back up even a step, tuck his tails and run for the fucking hills. I grabbed the back of his head and pulled my head back at the same time. Smashing my forehead into his,

147

headbutting him hard as fuck. I didn't feel shit from the impact, my adrenalin pumping at a fucking hundred.

This nigga had disrespected every fucking person I loved in the same damn sentence. And he did it in a way trying to threaten me. Mentioning my unborn. I would be seeing his ass later.

He stumbled back dazed and fucking confused. His forehead split open, blood running down his face. He was only halfway on his feet, knees bent trying to stand the fuck back up. His shit was already swelling up.

"What the fuck?" He yelled out, drawing the attention from the customers that were eating who hadn't noticed the commotion until now.

"I'll see you later nigga." I replied still calm and cold.

Drew intervened and grabbed his arm. The nigga tried to shake off the grip on his arm. But Drew lifted his shirt enough for the fuck nigga to see wasn't no games being played in here. I knew me or my man would kill this mothafucka in a heartbeat without a thought or contradiction. He gave in and Drew walked his ass back to the entrance of the restaurant. He shoved him out the door, where one of the niggas Drew brought with him from Houston, took his ass away and out of sight.

Drew walked back over to the table. Nya and Jolie both stood up. I guess our meal was over with now. Jolie pulled my boy in for a hug acting like a girlfriend to him. Nya stood up, placed her arm across my shoulders and forced my ass to turn around and look at her. She ran her hand over the small gash on my own forehead, that I could feel now.

When niggas like that pussy came at me, I didn't do much thinking it was fucking "GO". My automatic responses took over and the other side of me came out. This is how the streets made me. I wouldn't have the shit any other way though. It was kill or get killed point blank period.

Nya wiped the small trickle of blood away, then gently kissed my forehead by pulling my head down more. This shit probably looked weird as fuck to anyone looking at us. But I didn't give a fuck. If my bitch wanted to tend to her man, she sure the fuck could. It felt good as hell to be taken care of by a real ass woman.

"Damn, I love when you do that shit." She said in my ear before letting my head come back up to my full height.

"That's 'cus your my bitch." I shook my head at her. She really was just like my ass so I couldn't say shit.

Nya's smile turned into a frown out of nowhere. She clutched her stomach and leaned over. I reached out, giving my arm for support as she scrunched up her face. Her breathing getting heavy.

"I need to go to the hospital. It's time bae."

"You sure? No dessert then?" I joked.

"Nigga you better get our shit, Let's go!" She got louder as her face tensed up again. I guess she was having contractions. Damn there goes that fucking mouth again.

"Okay baby mama. Let's go. You know this nigga don't understand shit. His hardheaded ass trying to pop jokes and stuff. Boy bye." Jolie came over and brushed me off, helping Nya walk ahead to the exit.

Drew gave me a look like damn, he knew I was in for it now. I still laughed and followed my ass right behind the two females talking shit about me. I guess humor wasn't the way to go with this shit. But how was I supposed to know. I was about to be a mohtafuckin' father. That shit hit me after we got in the car and I started driving, speeding through the city streets.

After 7 hours in the delivery room, Kwamir Harris arrived. That shit lit a nigga's heart up. It was hard as hell to watch, but all worth it. When the doctor asked if I wanted to cut the damn umbilical cord, I hesitated. I wasn't scared of shit, but this shit was something that terrified me. Now my life was really on the line for my seed. Who thought a gangsta like me, could make something so fucking perfect. Damn I really lucked the fuck up with finding Nya. Her ass wasn't going no fucking where.

Drew

At lunch shit might have seemed all sweet and like everything was good between me and Jolie and for the most part it was true. We had never argued or had any damn problems. That was until earlier when I hit raw and busted in her.

Jolie freaked the fuck out on me for that shit. It wasn't on purpose, I got caught up with how good her pussy was. I couldn't understand why she made it such a big ass deal. But there was more to it than she was telling me earlier. She wasn't honest about everything. I knew she was holding some shit back behind it.

I wasn't in any hurry to get her ass pregnant. I mean damn, she just had a baby a few months ago and was raising 2 kids. That shit was enough on her, for now. Eventually I would want to officially take her off the market and marry her. I was the type of man that looked ahead. A lot of mothafucka's in my position took shit day by day. And that shit was probably smarter. But it was in my nature to plan shit out ahead. That was another thing me and Jolie had in common. She did the same exact thing with her life.

Not that I had been ready to settle down with any of the bitches I was fucking with before, but I always saw myself having a family one day. Now I moved up the ladder in the streets and my position was a lot fucking higher. Not having to be in the streets the same way I was before. I thought about the shit more and more. Jolie was fucking perfect. She was bad as fuck, a freak in the bed with fire pussy. She was even the truth when it came to parenting.

She was finally someone I could bring home to my mom and be proud to have on my arm. So for her to flip the fuck out on me, had me questioning what the hell was really the problem. It had to be some more shit behind her reaction. The kids were with the babysitter but Jolie wanted to pick them up before Nya had the baby. We went straight to the hospital from the restaurant to be there for her. But it seemed that the baby wasn't coming right away, so we headed out to pick the kids up.

She was just gonna bring them back to hospital with us. I didn't mind being around her children. Hell, in my mind I already stepped up to be their father myself now that my man was gone. It was another way I could hold Buck down making sure they were set the fuck up.

"You good now?" I asked driving back to her place.

"I'm not trying to go there with you right now Drew!" Jolie said still with that fucking attitude.

I nodded my head looking straight the fuck ahead. I wasn't gonna beg my bitch to do a damn thing. She was overreacting and had me questioning if she was really in this shit for the long haul. Now she was pissing me off.

"You know me, and you know I'm not going for that shit. You got a problem, you need to speak on it and not push that shit under the rug. So tell me, what's really the big deal? I slipped up, but damn what's up? You don't want to have my baby? You second guessing shit? Don't have me out here thinking you're the one and you're not even being honest."

Since day fucking 1 I kept shit a hundred with Jolie. Even when I knew she was still getting over Buck, I didn't hold back. I let her know I had feelings for her and kept my distance. She was the one that came back seeking out a relationship with me after it was all said and done. I didn't push her into a damn thing. I wasn't gonna stay with her ass if she felt like I was fucking things up for her or if she felt pressured into shit. Fuck that. There was still plenty of bitches trying to get my attention every single day. None of them compared to Jolie in my eyes. But I wouldn't let a bitch play me out either.

"It's just some shit I'm dealing with still. I want to be with you, I do. But sometimes I feel like it's a betrayal to Buck. I was so in love with him, planning a life with him. Now you're here and he's not. I miss him so much still and I don't know, damn. How can I be happy, when the love of my life is gone? It's shit like today that reminds me of times with him too. My head is still all fucked up behind this shit. I care about you, but how can I get past him?"

"You gotta make up your mind whether you're gonna live in the past or move on and let go. I'm not saying forget, but you deserve to be happy whether it's with me or the next man on some real shit." I parked the car in her driveway and used my hand to turn her head, to look at me.

Her eyes were filled with tears. The sadness was back. This shit was fucking with me bad. I loved this woman, even though I hadn't told her yet. But I had to make sure she was ready to receive that love. I couldn't expect her to move at my pace, but I couldn't set myself up to be fucked over. I wasn't built to play second to any man even the memory of one.

Jolie needed to decide if she could ever move past Buck and start looking at me like the love of her life. That was the only way shit would work between us. She had to let go of the life they would never have together. Until then, I needed to pull back and let her get her shit together. I didn't blame her, I wasn't mad, but I would be lying if the shit she said didn't fucking sting. It was a hard ass pill to swallow knowing my bitch wasn't really my bitch at all. She was one foot in and one foot out of this relationship.

"Look at me." She brought her gaze up and met my eyes. "I love you and I got you. But you need time to heal on your own."

Her eyes looked worried and she didn't answer what I said. I wanted her to say that shit back, that she loved me and knew she wanted to be with me. That this shit was real and she saw a future with me. But she didn't. That only verified I was doing the right thing.

Jolie leaned forward and started sucking on my bottom lip. Then stuck her tongue in my mouth kissing rough and urgent as hell. I didn't object and kissed her ass back. Her hand found my dick and she slid it down the waistband of my jeans, working it back and forth. Everything she was doing was intense, like she needed this shit right now. Maybe she was scared I was gonna leave for good. Or maybe she was worried that she knew deep down that she would never get over Buck and this was it for us.

Either way, I gave in and met her intensity with my own. I could never say "no" to this woman. She had my fucking heart now. I reached out, cupping her big ass titties, rubbing my thumbs over her nipples peeking through the thin fabric of her red shirt.

The sun was just going down, making it so I could still see every part of her sexy ass body. I stopped fucking around and lifted her ass up and over the center console onto my lap. Straddling my lap grinding on my shit, still fully clothed. I rubbed over every part of her body. Then lifted her shirt over her head. I wanted to enjoy as much of her fucking body as possible and the car wasn't doing the shit for me. So I opened my car door and picked her up again setting her down on the pavement before getting out of the whip myself.

She had that same worried ass look, while she put her hands on her thick ass hips, standing in front of me in her red lace bra, her body calling to me. That shit was fire red, sexy as fuck. I hurried up and picked her ass right back up. She wrapped her juicy thighs around my waist as I carried her over to the side of the house behind the privacy fence she had up.

Just behind the privacy fence I let her down and watched as she scooted her jeans down hopping slightly until they were over her feet. She kept her socks on and came up out of her sneakers to get them off. Standing in front of me was her fat pussy showing through the lace thong she had on. Her skin seemed to glow out here in the dimming light with the shit she had on standing out in contrast to her caramel skin. Her hair color matching the red in them.

Fuck it, I turned her around abruptly pushing her the few steps over to the side of her house. She braced herself with her hands pressed out against the siding for support. She smelled so fucking good. I came in closer, placing kisses on the nape of her neck. Her body instinctively came back in response closing the distance between us. Her ass resting against my dick now that it was free from my pants. My boxers pulled down just enough.

We could have gone inside or waited but we both wanted to fuck. No thinking, no waiting, I wanted to feel her pussy gripping my dick right the fuck now. Jolie leaned her head slightly to side allowing me to suck and lick more on the bitch.

I lowered my hand, keeping the other around her waist bringing her further back. Moving her thong to side, sliding my dick in.

She caught her loud moan by clamping down her mouth biting her lip. That shit made her pussy do the same mothafuckin' thing.

I forced her to work her hips with my hand on her stomach in control. She got into the shit, popping that pussy on my dick, moving faster to the rhythm I set. I bent my knees going deeper. Keeping her thong out of the way, to give me unrestricted access.

Jolie started throwing her shit back on her own adjusting to my size. She went to fucking work, lowering herself more leaned over against the house and tooted that fat ass up in the air. With her ass up, back arched I let her do her thing, fully twerking putting the pussy on me.

"Ahhhh, yes, Drew, you better…" She tried to whisper getting louder with every word she let out.

I took that as my cue and switched shit up, giving her slow strokes. Pushing into Jolie's pussy deeper feeling the pressure from the base hitting the tip of my dick. Her ass tried to run from the mothafucka going further into the side of the house and raising up to her tiptoes trying to change the angle. I knew I was hitting her G spot. Her body stopped moving, more cum coating my dick. She was so fucking wet that the noises from my dick sliding in and out could be heard. In the fading light I watched her ass shake and gripped her hips harder.

I lifted her ass right the fuck up like I did earlier but with my dick still planted inside of her and her facing away. Then walked her over to the swinging bench on the side of us. I eased myself down with her on top. She knew what the fuck to do.

As soon as I was seated, she placed her palms on my thighs and rode that shit out in reverse. Her thong was so stretched out that the bitched stayed in place up on her hip and I could enjoy the fucking view of her ass bouncing. I reached around grabbed her titties and forced her to stop fucking around and come all the way down each time she moved up and down.

She screamed out and cummed again. This time I felt my own nut rising in time and lifted her up off my dick just before cum shot out landing on my stomach and some on her ass from below. This quickie was good as fuck and our bodies said all the shit we didn't or wouldn't.

I loved this woman. But after tonight I was staying out in Houston. I needed to give her time and space and let her figure her own shit out. Jolie must have sensed my mood shift because when she came back over from picking our pants up and shaking them out, she gave me a sad ass look. Then placed a gentle kiss on my lips. The shit was like some movie shit but it was awkward.

I told myself that I wasn't doing this shit for me, that I was doing it for her. But either way come morning she wouldn't see my ass again anytime soon.

Nya

I reached out and picked up my son, cradling him closer in my arms. Fuck what everyone said, pregnancy was hard as hell and labor was even worse. I thought my pussy was being torn in two for real this time. Even though Saint's dick was big as fuck, nothing prepared your body for a whole baby to come out. It was everything I would have never wanted to experience. But looking down and holding my son it was all worth it. I would do that shit a thousand times over to be able to hold him in my arms.

Kwamir was so damn little. I was still getting used to holding him and caring for him. He did fine latching on and breastfeeding which I was initially worried about. I wanted to keep shit as natural as possible but I was a realistic bitch and if shit didn't go that way I would just go with it. The same way I wanted to have a natural birth without an epidural. That shit went out the window after the contractions came. I was hollering "epidural" so damn fast. But even with that shit, the pain still came back right before giving birth. If that wasn't some bullshit, I didn't know what was.

Jolie and Drew came in one at a time to see Kwamir so each of them could stay in the waiting room with the babies. Even though so much shit was going on and my body felt like it got ran over by a damn truck, I still noticed their moods were both off. Way different than this afternoon. But right now all my energy was going towards caring for an actual another human being that I was responsible for. Yeah, this shit still freaked me the hell out. I didn't know if I would be a good mother even with saint and everyone else's encouragement.

I was actually relieved when Jolie said good-bye and left after holding her nephew and loving on him doing the most. She needed to get home and have some time to relax and get their own children to sleep. Drew was supposed to be there to make shit better for her. So his ass better not be stressing her. Or it was gonna be some problems from me. He was cool and all but he wasn't family yet that was for damn sure. I was rocking with Jolie for life.

I laid back down in the hospital bed, still cradling Kwamir in my arms. I couldn't seem to put him down for long. Every time I put laid him in the plastic hospital portable shit, I felt nervous as hell like wondering if he was still breathing and shit. The anxiety that came with this mother shit already was some other level shit.

I closed my eyes, looked to my side where Saint was passed out in between two hospital chairs pulled together. Acting like he went through the damn ordeal himself. I smiled at the sight and laid further back against the pillows fully content with my life.

Out of fucking nothing came this small beautiful family of mine. With Terrell, Saint, Jolie and now Kwamir my heart was full.

---

1 month came and went in the blink of a damn eye. Christmas was a blur since Kwamir was born right before and everything in our lives was focused around him right now. My life consisted of sleepless nights, changing diapers, baths and altogether just being worn out. Don't get me wrong I was still grateful as fuck. But this motherhood shit was no joke.

I had only been out of the house a few times and today was the first day I was taking Kwamir with me other than to his few doctor appointments. I was overprotective as hell with him and believed in some of the old saying about taking newborns out around germs and shit. I didn't have shit to complain about because Saint was home more and helped me a lot with our son. On top of that Terrell even stepped up and helped at times. That shit was saying a lot for an 18 year old senior in high school. That let me know I had done something right with him.

Today I was going over to Jolie's to spend some girl time with her. We stayed talking on the phone for hours every day, but only saw each other a few times when she came to see Kwamir. She was caught up in her own shit right now. Since Drew and her had cooled things off. She tried to act like the shit wasn't fucking with her as bad as it was, but I knew her ass and could tell she was really in love with that man. Even if she didn't want to admit it to herself.

Since it was the weekend, I planned to make this shit an event. Jolie agreed to cook a big meal getting everyone together for a family dinner. She was having the babysitter come over to give us adults a few hours of reprieve and watch them in the other rooms. I damn sure wasn't comfortable leaving Kwamir with anyone yet but having him in the other room was another thing. He was still right up under my watch if needed.

He was on a bottle tonight, because my ass was about to drink. The doctor still hadn't cleared me for sex and I honestly didn't know if I would even be ready in the next few days after I went for my 6 week checkup. My pussy was still sore as hell and I couldn't even think about Saint's dick without cringing right now. Don't get me wrong I missed the way he sexed my body and the way he made me feel. I thought about the shit all the time, but now my body and mind was somewhere else. Saint was always patient with me but I knew my nigga and he was getting restless.

He was a sexual ass man, and he already let it be known that he couldn't wait for my doctor's appointment next week. I hadn't told him how I was really feeling because I didn't want him to take that shit personally. So for right now I was avoiding the damn subject.

"What's up man, you're looking fresh today? Where you going?" Terrell came in the kitchen and picked Kwamir up talking to him like he understood the shit he was saying. Both Terrell and Saint talked to my baby like he was older than he was. Kwamir just sat there staring and smiling at them like he understood. It was so ridiculous.

I had him dressed in a onesie sweat suit, black gold and gray. With some matching Jordan booties. I had to admit, my son was so cute for real. Like his little ass could be in one of those baby commercials, with his adorable dimples he took after Jolie and his smile and eyes like his daddy. The only thing he got form me that I could tell so far was his skin complexion. He was darker than Saint and took after my coloring. His ass was gonna have all the little girls after him, but if it was up to me he would be

166

respectful and stay the hell away from them for as long as possible.

I caught myself smiling at the sight before me.

"We got a family dinner tonight over at Jolie's. Be there around 7:00." I instructed Terrell.

"Bet. Can I bring somebody?" That shit caught my attention.

"Who you wanna bring baby brother?" I asked eyebrows raised.

"I want ya'll to me my girl, shit is... I mean things are, getting more serious and I know you'll like her."

"She better not be a lil' hoe 'Rell. You know I raised you better than that. And there better not be no damn babies. You got some shit you gotta do first, before you become a father. So don't get no ideas."

"I know, I know, It ain't that serious. A nigga got dreams too. It's just she's the real thing. She's going to college in the fall just like me. You ain't gotta worry sis."

I stared his ass down. "Alright, bring her. But you know, none of us got filters. So she better be prepared. We're your family so if she's really down, you'll find out tonight."

I know I was being hard on him, but nobody went easy on a young black man in this world. So that shit got taught at home. I loved my brother to death and wasn't gonna

167

let some girl bring him down. Hopefully she was everything he thought she was. Terrell usually had good judgment and he never brought any of his other little girlfriends around. I wasn't naive, I knew he had the bitches sweating him.

I walked over to where he was standing on the other side of the counter and took Kwamir from his arms, settling him back into his car seat on top of the counter top. Then gave my brother a hug.

"What was that for?" He asked when I pulled back.

"You done grew up on me. But don't forget I always got you, bruh."

This was that sentimental shit I had been on lately. But I was speaking nothing but straight facts. Even if Terrell fucked up and did some shit I didn't agree with, I would always have his back and make sure he was good. That was what the fuck family was for.

I grabbed the car seat and headed out the door. Immediately hit with the cool January air, clutching my sweater closer I hurried the fuck over to my Benz. After getting Kwamir situated in the back, I headed the short distance over to Jolie's.

On the way, I couldn't' shake the feeling of someone watching me. I even checked my review and side view mirrors over and over, but there wasn't a damn car in sight on the few streets in between my place and Jolie's. By the time I pulled into her driveway, I convinced myself that I was paranoid as hell from barely coming out of the house. This new worrying shit, was what I attributed to having a newborn.

I went ahead and got my ass up in the house as soon as possible. I wasn't about this cold shit. I shivered and looked down at Kwamir's innocent perfect face after closing the front door back behind myself. Damn he reminded me of his daddy, giving me looks like him and all. That discerning shit and disapproval one, like when we first ran back into each other in Houston outside the strip club.

At the time that shit irked my damn soul. But now, I knew that it was my saving grace. The light at the end of the tunnel I had been needing in my life.

"Bitch where you at?" Jolie hollered out from the dining room table across the house.

Of course when I walked up she was sitting down drinking her tea and reading some kind of shit on her kindle. Jolie consumed herself with reading all the damn time when we were kids. She was a true book worm. Now that she wasn't teaching she said it was how she stimulated her mind. I knew she was just doing more of it since Drew wasn't around. When his ass was dicking her down, there wasn't a book in sight. Not when Buck was here either.

"Okay nasty! I know your ass ain't reading that shit in the middle of the damn afternoon, when we got shit to do." I said playing with her. But for real Jolie loved those Hood Love books that were filled with plenty of sex.

"Whatever, I just wanted to finish this part. I'm good now."

"MMMMhhhhmmm. Whatever you say. But are you really good? It seems like you're missing something from your life."

"And what's that friend?" She asked with a look like she really wanted to know.

"You're missing some of that white meat." I said the last part louder and busted the hell out laughing.

Yes I was clowning her ass. But she had fucked up when she told me about the sex with Drew. Not that I wanted to think about that shit, but the way she made it sound, he was doing his damn thing laying that pipe on her. Now it was obvious she was missing him in more ways than one.

"Fuck you. You ain't right girl." She shewed me off with her hands and stood up walking her ass right the fuck away. Yup I was right. That was exactly her problem. Reading about all the shit she wished she was doing with Drew. That was what the hell she was up to.

She confided in me how he was cooling on her right now since she told him she wasn't over Buck and didn't know if she would ever be. The thing was she just didn't realize that she had the power to move on and put that love in the past. It wasn't something she couldn't control. That was where weakness came in. I firmly believed that when a bitch set her mind to something anything was possible. Feelings could be controlled.

For years I let my past control me and I shouldn't have given any of my time or energy to that shit. Yeah it helped me grow into the woman I was now. But shit could have went so much better for myself if I had let go. Hindsight was a bitch.

I followed Jolie into the kitchen helping her get the salad together from the ingredients and vegetables she pulled out from the fridge, while she put the baked macaroni in the oven.

"Jolie, stop wasting your time for real. One love don't got replace the other. Choose to let Buck go, and move on with Drew. He's your future hunny." I said more serious.

"How though?' she sounded exasperated.

"Stop comparing them. Live in the now. The feeling you have now. I'm not saying forget Buck altogether. But force yourself to think about Drew instead until he's the one who's always on your mind. I know it ain't easy. But if you don't try you're gonna be stuck loving a dead man and that shit will hold you back from being happy. Buck wouldn't want that shit for you or the kids. You deserve to be happy."

"I don't know..."

"Well some more advice, you better decide because you know how many bitches were waiting for your place? I bet those hoes are already up trying to live your life with your man. Don't think for a minute that Drew's fine paid ass ain't getting some pussy just because you ain't getting no dick. He just might fuck around and find another bitch who wants to love his ass back."

"The fuck he will." She said fiercely while stirring the gumbo fast as fuck. Yeah the shit I said got to her. But that was what I wanted, her to realize that time wasn't guaranteed. Tomorrow wasn't promised for a mothafuckin' person. She needed to get her house in order.

We continued fixing the dishes in silence, so I turned on Tidal and started my playlist. Most of my shit was straight rap. That was just the type of bitch I was. But

172

when some of my old songs played the mood changed. As soon as Deborah Cox's "Nobody's Supposed to Be Here" came on Shit got real. Jolie hurried the hell up out the kitchen with her cell phone in her hand. I bet anything her ass was going to call Drew.

I smiled like a damn Cheshire cat when she came back a few minutes later smiling herself. That was my friend. She lightly punched my arm on her way back over to the sink.

"What?!" I laughed.

"You ain't slick."

"But I see you smiling now though, so who ain't slick?." We both laughed, as I poured us each a glass of the sweet red wine on the counter.

The doorbell rang and Jolie went to get it. She brought the babysitter over to where I was and introduced us. She was probably around 19. Only a little younger than us but with a whole lot younger demeanor. We were some grown women and from the minute I looked at her she seemed like the typical college girl.

After the greeting, Jolie took her to the living room where the babies were still sleeping and told the sitter that BJ was in his room watching a movie. She went ahead and picked up the babies one at a time gently, taking them in the back room with her.

I took another sip of the wine watching her interact with my son. This shit was gonna take some getting used to. But if Jolie vouched for the bitch and I was right here, I would get past the paranoia I was feeling all damn day.

"Thank you, Malaysia." Jolie said.

The girl smiled at us both, "no worries, thank you for the opportunity to watch these beautiful babies." She said through an unusual accent. She was light skinned like Jolie, pretty and obviously from up North.

The babies stayed quiet so that shit meant they were still sleeping at least for now. Me and Jolie both got back to work. Her in the kitchen and me straightening up the living room, moving some of the baby things out of the way. The front door opened and Saint walked in looking like a tall glass of some good ass dark liquor. He was so damn smooth and sexy. If only the rest of my body caught the hell up with my mind.

This nigga had me standing here midair with a pillow in hand, drooling for a minute. No matter how many damn times I got to look at him, the effect was till polarizing. He walked over to me with the same boss ass demeanor, matching his look.

"What's got your tongue shawty?" Damn even the way he said tongue was sexy. He came close and wrapped his strong arms around my lower waist resting his hands in their usual place, right on my ass.

"Stop playin' with me daddy. You know how we're rocking when the time comes." I promised.

This shit was still crazy that as much as my mind was telling me yes, my body was saying no. So I slyly put some distance between us and used my hand to push back against his chiseled chest. I really needed to get my shit together and put my silly ass apprehensions aside. This upcoming Monday I was going to the doctors and that shit was what it was. I was just gonna have to bite the bullet and put out for my nigga, no matter what my body was telling me. I damn sure wasn't gonna let another bitch tempt him.

"Damn it smells good as fuck in here." He followed behind me into the kitchen keeping himself pressed close the whole way, dick tucked right between my ass cheeks. He was soft, but the mothafucka was big enough to feel the pressure.

Saint went over to the pots on the stove, lifting the lids, trying to get a taste of the gumbo. Jolie slapped his hand away. It was a wonder that me and her even knew how to cook. But with the internet and some family here and there for me as a kid I picked up on enough shit. Now I wasn't nowhere near as good as my own mother was. Jolie

175

could straight up throw down in the kitchen and she was completely self-taught. She always cooked for Saint even as kids. It was her small way of taking care of his ass, since he was the one who always took care of everything else. The first day he gave us some money off the block when he started hustling, her ass rushed to the store to pick up some food to cook.

It was shit like that that let you know you ain't come from shit. When the first thing on your mind is some damn food. But after that day they didn't go without again.

There was a knock at the door and Jolie hollered out loud as hell, "Come in" instead of walking over to get it. Terrell walked in with some beautiful young sister on his arm.

She looked like a good girl, but looks could be deceiving. We would find out more about her over dinner. I was gonna take it easy on her for now. Terrell always had good judgment, so I gave him the benefit of the doubt for now.

I heard babies crying. Jolie's hollering must have woke them up.

"Shit, well there goes that." She said putting down the towel she was wiping her hands with on the countertop. She was right behind me walking to the back room, to make sure out children were okay. It was a

176

mother's instinct. When I looked in the room, the sitter Malaysia was tending to them both one in each arm like they were twins. Joy calmed down first. I went the rest of the way into the room to go ahead and pick up Kwamir.

I sat down on the edge of the guest bed that I used to sleep on when I first got in town, and fed Kwamir a bottle out of his bag. The babysitter took the time to go get some water and food that Jolie offered her. Kwamir got his little ass back to sleep after the feeding and changing his diaper. The sitter still wasn't back yet, so I went ahead and left the door ajar, making my way down the hall back to the dining room.

As soon as I walked in, two mothafuckin' heads turned looking like somebody's ass was caught with their damn hand in the cookie jar. The damn babysitter was standing real fucking close, face to face with my baby daddy. Jolie was occupied with Terrell and his girlfriend in the kitchen, not paying attention to this scandalous shit here.

I felt my heart thumping through my chest, and I clenched my fists by my side. They weren't doing anything. But I got a feeling that they were both attracted to each other. Of course Saint's eyes and entire body language changed up when he noticed me. Too late nigga, I thought. Then the hoe smiled and said, "It was nice to meet you." I swear to God in my nigga's face. She attempted to walk past me with her food plate in hand pretending like I wasn't standing here. Not today.

I raised my arm, brought my elbow back and slammed my fist hard as fuck against the side of her eye before she made it by. I didn't play no hoe shit and disrespecting me just wasn't gonna happen period.

The girl stumbled to the side but regained some footing.

"What the fuck was that hoe? *It was nice to meet you.*" I said mocking her voice using two fingers on my hands to illustrate the fuckery. When I got mad like this it was like I wasn't in control. I knew what I was doing, but just didn't give a fuck.

"I.... I didn't mean anything. I don't know what..."

I lunged at her again stepping over the plate of food that spilled on the ground, grabbing for the bitch's throat. I pushed her up against the side of the dining room table.

"See what you not gonna do is play with a bitch like me. That disrespect shit will get you killed sweetie." I reached in my braids and pulled out my razor holding that shit up for her to see. I wanted her to realize how easily and quick I could hurt her.

Saint came up behind me and pulled me off the girl, coming to her damn rescue. Only pissing me the fuck off more. I didn't give a fuck if I was wilding out or not. My nigga should not be taking some other bitch's side.

"Get the fuck outa here." He told the Malaysia bitch over his shoulder, while he picked my ass up and carried me to the bathroom.

Saint

Here I was talking to the damn babysitter and there go Nya's crazy ass. Fighting a bitch, tearing shit up like she didn't have no damn sense. Pulling out her blade was way over the fucking top and uncalled for.

I picked her small ass up and toted her right the fuck back to the bathroom, setting her down on the front of the counter. She could have a damn seat with all that unnecessary shit.

I knew my bitch was all the way out there for a nigga. But this shit wasn't serious at all. The hoe was just saying hello. She might've wanted more than that from me, but there was a gang of hoes that stayed on my dick every day. That shit came with the territory. Nya knew this.

Shit, she had seen the women throw themselves at me with her right on my damn arm and never checked a girl the way she just did. So I needed to dead this shit right now. She couldn't be out fighting and threatening to kill any and all the women that tried to come at me.

"Calm all that shit down mane. You fuckin' 'round gonna kill somebody for no damn reason. What's your problem?" I stood over her arms folded in front across my chest checking her.

She looked up at me, still mad as hell huffing and puffing. Knowing her ass shouldn't be out here fighting and just had our son and shit. She copied my ass, folding her arms right over her chest too. But her ass spoke up with that fucking attitude and damn leg shaking fast. That was the same shit she always did when she was pissed off.

"That hoe deserved it. I seen the way ya'll were booed up. Then she's gonna try and be funny. You know me, and you know I will stomp a bitch, kill a bitch over you. Don't forget that shit nigga."

Damn, she was crazy as fuck. But knowing she went hard as hell for me was some real ass shit. I shook my head, "You gotta calm down with the shit. Your ass gonna be locked up. Who's gonna take care of the baby? You're a mother now. Handle your shit better shawty. That's all I'm saying."

Nya stood up trying to get up in my face, still fuming. "Nigga don't bring me being a mother into this. I saw the way you was looking at her. You been fucking around, since I can't give you any pussy?"

I held the back of her head and pulled her in for a deep tongue kiss. Yeah, she was reckless as fuck. But seeing her boss up, now trying to check me just made me want to remind her who she was really fucking with.

"Don't think I'm over the shit Saint." Nya said eyeing me when I let up.

She sat her sexy ass right the fuck back down, working her fingers to unbuckle my pants in the process. Nya sucked my dick every day since giving birth. Her head game was on point. She knew exactly how to handle the mothafucka like it was hers.

She gripped my dick in her small hand, then got down off the counter. Spitting on the mothafucka making it nasty, saliva dripping down. She took her time sliding her lips over the tip, down the length of my shaft. I moved my pelvis forward pushing myself further in, until my dick reached down the back of her throat. Every fucking inch.

Her juicy lips covered in spit moving up and down my dick was some shit a nigga loved to see. Nya enjoying eating my dick, made me get even harder. Then her ass started suctioning her jaws, cheeks coming in and out, making my dick fucking tingle.

"Damn." I reached down and cupped her left tittie under her shirt. Playing with her nipple through the fabric of her bra.

I started fucking her mouth, touching her tonsils with my hard strokes. Nya kept fucking working, using her tongue, letting more spit coat my dick swirling the bitch

182

around. Lubricating the mothafucka. She slid up and down faster. Gently juggling my balls in her hand. Looking up, not breaking eye contact.

Then she switched shit up and pulled back, holding my dick in her hand instead of her mouth, giving full attention to it. Turning her head sideways entrapping one then both of my balls in her wet mouth. Licking and sucking them one at a time. Taking her time on my most sensitive damn part. She knew what the fuck she was doing.

Nya came back up, opening her mouth again taking in only the tip of my dick. Sucking hard on the head not letting my full length enter all the way in between her lips. All at one she opened wide until her lips reached the base, throat closing down on my shit, sucking the fucking life out of me.

I tensed up, my dick jumping. I grabbed the back of her head, making her mouth move up and down my dick with force a few more times, until my cum shot out. Nya kept sucking, swallowing the way I liked. Kissing and sucking all over my dick even after I was finished.

"I love the way you taste. I love your dick." She said sweetly now. Her whole fucking tune changed from a few minutes ago.

I knew we were at my sister's house and had company, but I needed some pussy after that shit. Nya wasn't fully cleared to fuck yet, but what was one more day. I went ahead and pulled away enough to help her up, then slid her pants off. I lifted her ass up onto the counter.

"Wait... What? You know I..." I lowered myself and closed my mouth down on her clit before she could say shit else. It was finally time to return the favor.

I was back in fucking action, making love to her pussy with my mouth. Making sure to please her the way she had done me.

I latched on to her clit, and Nya's body fell in line. Moving to the rhythm of my fingers sliding nice and easy in and out of her. I knew she was scared of having sex after having our son. I knew this shit because I knew my bitch. I knew her mind and body even without her telling me shit. That was what the fuck being with your soul mate did.

I wanted to take my time, but I also knew Nya. I couldn't give her too much time to go back on this shit. It was the same way the first time we fucked. With her scary ass trying to back out. Nah, she wasn't backing out of shit. I was getting some of my pussy.

I let her clit go from in between my lips coming up and looking her dead in the eyes. I slid my dick inside her nice and slow the same way my hand was a minute before.

"Ahhhhh," She muffled the moan by biting her bottom lip, adjusting to being filled completely.

"Shhhhhh, I got you. Ease up bae." I whispered in her ear.

She threw her head back and closed her eyes while moving her hips with the slow motion of my light strokes.

I kissed all over the sexy ass skin of her neck, lifting her shirt up higher to expose her big ass titties spilling out of her bra. Switching between kisses, licking and sucking, moving in deeper with every stroke. She opened her eyes, following my gaze that was watching her pussy take the dick. I gripped her ass and started bringing her up off the counter. Going deeper. All the way to her stomach.

She started bringing her hips forward faster, working her pussy muscles. Fucking me back. With her eyes still trained right where our bodies were coming in contact, down at my dick sliding in and out of her. She took her hand and played with her clit. Her thumb and fingers applying more pressure on my dick as it came out. I lifted her legs up, locked the bitches with my elbows so she couldn't fucking move. It was my turn to take control.

"Saint, ahh!" She moaned intensely, trying to keep quiet.

"Let that shit go."

On fucking command her pussy closed on all sides pushing against my dick. But I kept moving hard, reaching my hands around to the back of her neck still locking her knees behind my elbows. She moaned out. After a few strokes her pussy rained on my fucking dick. Her body shaking and chest heaving up and down.

I let up and released the hold I had. Nya's body came unfolded and I stood back slightly only using my dick to fuck her pretty ass pussy. Nya wasn't having that shit though.

She came forward pulled my body to hers, pressing her titties against my chest and working her hips trying to get me to go deeper again. Her body tensed up with the intense strokes rubbing right on her clit in this position.

My nut came to the tip of my dick and I dug in one more time, busting deep in her pussy. With her juices flowing out at the same time. Her head buried into my shoulder biting down on my shoulder from the powerful orgasm.

I kissed her on the cheek and she turned her head, giving my ass a real ass kiss.

"How did you know I was scared?"

"What you mean?"

"Saint, I know you were taking it easy. I can read you too nigga. When you're inside me, it's like I'm in your head."

That was the same way shit was for me, "You ain't got nothing to be worried about with me. I got you. I wasn't 'bout to let your scary ass back out on me either. Just like the first time, trying to back out of shit, ol' bitch ass." I joked.

"Whatever nigga, it's not my fault you got another fucking leg trying to call it a dick. You know that shit ain't normal right." She said playfully.

"You good though?" I asked seriously, wanting to make sure she was alright. Last thing I wanted to do was hurt her somehow.

"I'm good bae. I'm gonna be sore as hell. But that ain't nothing new. For real though, don't let me catch you smiling in a bitch face again. I ain't the one nigga."

"Damn here you go right back on that shit."

"What? The dick was supposed to make me forget? I'm serious Saint. I told you from the jump I will end up going to jail behind you, so you better not fuck up."

"On God shawty, you ain't got shit to worry about. Just remember that shit you're spitting, 'cus I won't even be warning your ass. Ya'll both will be dead." I finished the last part as we finished putting on the last bits of our clothes.

We walked out of the bedroom after Nya wiped herself down and we checked ourselves over in the mirror. Nya in front like usual. When we got to the end of the hall, the mess that the girl Nya beat up was already gone. Jolie was picking up the remaining dishes on the table. Damn dinner was already done. We were only in the bathroom for about a half hour. The shit we just did was some record time for us.

Terrell and the girl he brought were chilling out in the living room, booed up with his arm around her. Sitting on the couch watching some shit on the big screen TV posted on the wall. I walked into the kitchen where Nya was now helping Jolie with the dishes instead of interrupting his shit.

"I'm gonna say this shit one time big brother. You need to go back in MY bathroom and wash off anything that's contaminated. I'm not playing with ya'll nasty hot asses." Jolie stared at me by turning her head over her shoulder. Trying to be all serious.

Nya chuckled and I smiled at my sister. I would go check behind us, but that was because I loved her ass. Anybody else I wouldn't have given a fuck how they felt. I knew she wasn't really mad either, she was just trying to act hard like usual. I was gonna do that shit, right after I ate this mothafuckin' plate of banging food that was calling my name on the counter.

"And by the way... Your man's coming in town tomorrow. We got a meet up with Juan, and I want ya'll to be there." I said between mouthfuls enjoying the fuck out of the food Jolie prepared.

There was nothing like some good ass home cooking. Nya did her thing in the kitchen, but my sister put her foot in the shit she made. I appreciated how she picked up how to cook on her own the way she did to make sure I was straight.

"What's the meeting about?" Nya's nosy ass asked.

"It's nothing for you to worry about. That shit will be handled separately. We're just going to lunch."

"Where we going to eat? And for your information, I already know DREW is coming in town." Jolie let it be known.

She didn't say it with any type of attitude which was better than the last time I mentioned his damn name. I didn't get in between their shit, but could tell she wasn't feeling him the past few weeks. His absence out here was noticed too. Then he told me he was making plans to stay in Houston permanently, so I figured there was really some shit going on.

That's why I warned her about seeing him at lunch. Juan wanted both the women to come and join us since his new wife was coming with him.

"We're just staying local, my spot."

Nya looked at me real intently and furrowed her eyebrows. Damn, she caught the meaning of the shit. But I refused to put her in any of this street shit right now. All she needed to do was sit her ass down and tend to our son and Terrell. And remember that her ass was supposed to be working towards being a lawyer. She couldn't be a criminal and a damn lawyer in training.

The shit was hot right now anyway with the other sides of town. I wasn't scared of none of the fallout from the price cuts and the end of the alliance. But I was smart enough to keep my family close.

In a few weeks those niggas would be so far buried in losses that they wouldn't be able to come back from the shit. Right now the mothafuckas were trying to lick their wounds and figure out a way to match the shit my team was pushing. But they couldn't fucking compete with the bitch ass connect they had. I knew that pussy Pedro too well. He wouldn't cut them deals or get them better shit because his ass couldn't.

He tried to act bigger than he was, when the truth was he was running the smallest cartel in Mexico. Now I had the backing of a bigger one, which was united with the biggest of them all. Shit was sweet on my end. After those bitch ass niggas fell in line or were out of the game all the way, then it wouldn't be a problem for Jolie or Nya to move however they wanted in the city. Across the bridge or wherever. But I wasn't risking shit with either of them. I didn't want them to know what was up, but I owed it to them to warn them that some shit was in the air.

"About that, you two gotta be on the lookout right now. Stay close to home, ya' heard meh. Shit's hot right now out 'cher."

They both nodded their heads and didn't ask any more questions. I appreciated that shit, especially since I knew Nya was biting her damn tongue probably so hard the bitch was ready to bleed. She was my mothafuckin' rider for real, a down ass bitch. But I wasn't they type of nigga to put her in shit when there was no need for it. I had this shit handled. If the time ever came where I needed her, I knew she would hold shit down.

Jolie

A damn month. That was how long it had been since I had seen my man. Yes, in my heart he was still mine. My palms were sweating, forehead clammy as I tried to sit cute waiting for him to walk in the entrance with my brother.

They were together earlier when I talked to Saint on the phone. I heard Drew's laugh in the background and got jealous of the shit. It didn't make any sense but I wanted that laugh back, in my presence enjoying shit with me.

He should have been struggling with the separation as much as I was. Yesterday after talking things over with Nya I realized she was right. We all had choices to make and I decided to let the past go. Not completely forget, but move on. I would always look back on the time I shared with Buck with appreciation and love. But I couldn't keep myself trapped in my head missing him, thinking about all of the "could have beens". I knew it wasn't gonna be easy. I was determined though to not look back and jump both feet in to this shit for real with Drew.

He told me he loved me the last night we were together. Along with leaving me with that bomb ass sex burning a hole in my mind night after night. I never did no shit like that. On the side of the house, outside. I never even thought I would like some shit so out in the open, but there was something about the possibility of someone seeing us. There was nothing like feeling wanted like that. I mean really wanted, like there wasn't another second that could go by without Drew putting his dick inside me.

Damn my man was so much of everything. It was hard to explain how I felt about him, but I knew when he said that "I was the one" he meant it. I knew that he was who I wanted to be with. The shit was crazy. My little light bright ass with a white man, when all I ever was attracted to was dark skin niggas. It was just something about Drew though. All the rules and thoughts of what I wanted were thrown out.

My throat got dry as I saw the door open. Of course we were back sitting in the same booth that we were at a month ago when we announced to my brother and Nya that we were a couple. This shit was déjà vu. And I damn sure wish we could have went to another place to eat.

Don't get me wrong, my brother's spot was off the chain and the food was good as hell. But this was the only restaurant we had been to lately. Now that he told us that wasn't about to change, I was cool on eating out after today. I might as well fix our food and have people over to my house when we wanted to catch up. As long as Nya didn't try and kill anybody else.

I reached out and took a small sip of the iced water in front of me to help my body relax. Drew was wearing a white shirt with a black logo across it and a fitted black NY Yankees hat. He wore his usual expensive ass white gold Rolex and some Timbs. His ass was crazy to me, not having a jacket on in this weather. But he always forgot about shit, except when I reminded him. That's how good we were together.

His eyes met mine from across the floor. He didn't look away. When I called yesterday he was trying to be short with me at first. He was polite, but distant. Now looking at him there was definitely still more feelings behind his intense stare.

He walked behind Saint towards the table. The two of them sat down. Nya put her phone down on the table, reaching her hand out across the table. Resting her palm on Saint's arm, rubbing it gently. My girl loved my damn brother's dirty drawers. She was the strongest bitch I knew, except when it came to his ass.

I was avoiding looking directly at Drew now that he was right next to me. But once Nya and Saint were kissing, catching up with each other, I turned my head letting my eyes fall on him again.

His dark eyes were looking right at me. I noticed they had a gray tone that I never paid attention to before. His olive complexion looked smooth as hell and he had let his beard grow out some more. The whole thing gave him an even more boss ass look. He rubbed his hand through his fresh lined up goatee and then put his cold hand right on my thigh.

The heat from my legs didn't mind the cold from the contact. I was hot all over. My pussy was calling to him already. His ass just looked at me like he knew exactly what the hell I was caught up thinking about.

"You miss me?" He had the damn nerve to ask.

Knowing I did. Knowing I called yesterday because I wanted to make things right.

I nodded my head, "Did you miss me?"

Instead of avoiding answering he leaned in close to my ear, breath on my neck making every nerve in my body respond. "Too fucking much. You with me now?" He pulled back.

I knew what he meant. "All the way." I answered as boldly as I felt about really doing this thing.

Don't get me wrong, I had wanted Drew for months. I didn't want to lose him as a friend or someone I could depend on. That was why I decided to act on my feelings that were developing for him initially all those months ago. But now I was doing this shit for real. I was giving him my heart. I loved him, the same way he loved me. I hadn't told him, but I would when the time was right.

I wanted to do this shit with him different. I wanted to live this shit out day by day, going full force without any regrets or second guessing. He began rubbing the inside of my thigh through my jeans. I loved every motion Drew made as long as he was touching me. He made me feel secure.

Juan and his new wife walked in a few minutes later. Looking at the woman I could tell she wasn't like me and Nya. No matter how big Saint got, or now Drew for that matter, me and her would always be down to earth. Just two girls from the hood who kept shit real and had some sense along with a fat bank account.

This woman looked straight boujiee. I always tried to get to know people before I decided what was what with them. Maybe she was a good person and I was jumping to conclusions. She was dressed in designer shit from head to toe and looked like her ass, breasts and some of her face were paid for. To me all that extra surgery shit was not a good look, but to each their own.

Juan didn't seem to mind. Just like a lot of these corny ass niggas. I still didn't like or trust Juan. He may be coming to the rescue playing the brotherly role now, but to me the shit was all fraud as hell. He never came around before Saint made a name for himself in the streets. It was like we were all beneath him before. Now he wanted to have lunch and shit. Everybody else could be fooled but I still felt the same way I did when I saw him at the hospital back when Saint was shot up.

After greeting them, I realized my initial thoughts about his wife were right.

"I love your earrings, and your necklace". She doted on the simple diamonds studs and necklace I usually wore. They were nice but nothing special. Clean, expensive, not over the top. She added, "I have a pair of diamonds in too. Look at that! Juan bought them for me last week." She tried showing them off to impress me. Or to try and make me feel less than, since hers were three times the size of mine.

This woman just didn't know me. I laughed at bitches like her. But to keep the peace, I smiled and nodded my head. Saint wanted us to have lunch so I would be nice. Hopefully the hoe didn't say anything to Nya because she wouldn't hold back from saying what she wanted no matter the time or place.

Nya gave me a knowing look as I said "thanks", smiling at me while she took a drink of her red wine.

We had decided on a bottle of Cabernet with our lunch. I ordered a chef salad and soup of the day. Everybody else wanted some kind of seafood dish at our table. But I wanted something different today. I was feeling like a whole lot of new and different was what I needed.

"So brother, tell me how are things?" Juan asked Saint directly in his slight Spanish accent.

His question was unexpected since Saint said he would talk about business later when he told us about the meeting yesterday. He went along with it somewhat.

"Things are good here. It's the other shit I want to discuss when we finish here. We can talk about that shit in my office, while the women stay here and enjoy dessert." He set his napkin down and leaned back.

Nya was eyeing Juan just like I was.

"Oh, but baby can't you stay and talk about whatever it is here. You know I miss you when you're gone."

Was this bitch serious? I had never seen such a clingy woman with an important man before. Juan was in the black market. All underground shit. It wasn't a secret to any of us at this table. Either she didn't know or she didn't care that certain things couldn't be talked about out in the open. Anyone with sense knew listening ears were everywhere. I damn sure knew why my brother didn't want to discuss things out here on the floor.

Then Juan actually looked at Saint and gave him a shrug as if acting defeated. Asking without "asking", if they could go over the shit out here. The way he was acting all nonchalant was strange as hell. Maybe he was just caught up in the honeymoon phase of his marriage and had temporarily lost his damn mind.

"I'll be in the office, ya' heard me." Saint said standing up.

That was just like him. Saint never repeated himself. He said what the hell he meant and meant what he said. Even though Juan wasn't up under Saint and was supposed to be a boss in his own right, his ass stood up and followed behind my brother.

Drew stayed behind for a minute. Taking the opportunity to move his hand from my thigh to my face. Turning my head with his hand, giving me a kiss. Nothing much, but this what some of what I missed. Drew was attentive and made me feel wanted. I never had to question him or the way he felt. He was a real ass man with his shit. It made me feel like I could be on some grown ass woman shit with him.

I watched my man walk away. Damn I couldn't wait to spend some much needed alone time with him later. Nya's ass was smiling sitting back in the booth eyes glued to me, like I had some big ass secret to share.

"I see you bitch! Go 'head hunny."

"Whatever, girl." I cut my eyes over at the other company at our table.

No way was I talking about my personal life with practically a stranger in our midst. Nya wasn't gonna do it either. She just couldn't hold back from making a small comment though. That was what best friends were for.

"So... how long have you and Juan been married?" I asked Juan's wife, changing the subject. Trying to make small talk. It was awkward as hell. Besides how fake this bitch was, she rubbed me wrong the wrong way for whatever reason. Nya hadn't even bothered to greet the woman. She didn't fuck with hardly anyone and didn't try and have manners either. So I knew she wasn't feeling the girl. But neither of us really had a reason. So I was still trying to be cordial.

"Listen, ladies. We don't have to pretend. I can tell you two don't like me and to be honest, you're not exactly... the type of women I'm usually around either. So don't waste your breath. We can enjoy our dessert without the small talk."

Oh hell no. This bitch really tried to come at us with that better than you attitude. Thinking she could talk down to us. Nya mean mugged her and reached for her purse. I knew she was either reaching for a gun or her blade. Both of those wouldn't be good with a restaurant full of people. My friend was always a hot head, but since having Kwamir she was on a different level with it. And this hoe definitely wasn't worth the effort.

I reached out and grabbed Nya's hand while it was still inside her coach purse that was now on her lap. I pulled her up with me instead, as I stood to my feet. Fuck this stuck up bitch. She could finish her dessert by herself. We didn't need to sit with her a second longer. We went ahead and took our asses right the hell over to one of the tables by the window and called the waitress over to bring us our food over here.

When I looked back at our usual booth, Juan's wife was looking at us with a mixture of hate and disbelief. Maybe she was used to talking down to people and getting away with it. That shit might have worked for her in Puerto Rico. But she came across the wrong ones for that. She was lucky she wasn't hemmed up, knocked out on the floor, or staring down the barrel of a gun right now. I saved her ass.

Once my cheesecake arrived and Nya's molten chocolate cake with ice cream got to our table, we began eating our desserts in peace like the hoe suggested. Having a good time.

"Can you believe that stuck up hoe? She's lucky you saved her damn life. I was about to teach her ugly ass a lesson."

"I bet your were friend. You got to calm that shit down Nya for real, for real." I told her giving her a hard stare. She needed to think about the consequences more and hold back from spazzing out. Now more than ever. Kwamir needed his mother on this side.

"Yeah, yeah I hear you. But ANYWAY, I see you and your white chocolate are good again."

"Oh my God, I can't with you! "White chocolate". Where the hell you come up with that from?"

"I mean he's obviously white, but he got that chocolate in him now, or wait... is he in the chocolate now?" She busted out laughing loud enough that a few people turned in our direction. She thought her corny ass joke was so funny. I did laugh right along with her though.

"And he do be all up in this chocolate, let me tell you." I added for emphasis since she wanted to go there.

"Ewwwww" I don't wanna hear it.

"Whatever! Shut up. You're the one that started it. What can I say though, love makes you act crazy sometimes. I was afraid before, but after you rapped that real shit to me yesterday, I knew where my heart was and what I needed to do..I called his ass up and now we're really about to do this. No fear or holding back." I confessed getting serious.

"I'm so happy for you. You deserve a man like Drew. And no lie, he is kinda fine for a white boy. Ya'll cute or whatever." She joked again.

"Leave my baby alone. He is more than fine."

Loud clanking of heels started peddling in the direction of our table. We were seated close to the entrance next to a window. Nya's eyes got that same mean ass look in them as they had when she was staring at Juan's wife. I turned around and saw the reason for her changed expression.

Coming up to our table was one of Drew's ex ratchet hoe's. I swear I wasn't trying to be messy with my shit in the streets. I didn't want to deal with any of the bullshit fighting I used to have to do behind Buck. My man was my man point blank period.

"Not today! Don't do it." Nya said loud enough to be heard. Not all out yelling in Saint's restaurant. See her ass could have some restraint. I knew it.

Of course these hoes just were not smart today. The bitch continued coming forward, walking all the way up to the side of the table.

"Let your little scary ass friend talk that shit then. He really got you gassed up. But Drew will be back calling me like he was last weekend. Bet that shit." The hoe said twisting her neck and using her hands. Clapping in my face at the end of her rant.

"Who's scary?" I stood up.

I didn't say shit else. It was on. I reached out, snatching the big ass fake hoops out of the bitch's ears. She screamed out in pain, reaching up to feel the damage as blood trickled down from the torn holes.

I dropped the cheap pieces of jewelry on the floor, turned back around and laid a hundred on the table. Then started walking towards the back office. It was time for me to get the hell out of here. There had been enough damn drama for one day. I wasn't technically a teacher anymore, so charges weren't anything for me. But it wasn't in my character to all out fight if I could avoid it.

I felt like this was some juvie shit, for back in high school. Or for those drunk

204

nights Buck tested my gangster with some random hoe. It wasn't worth the damn trouble, especially over some trash like the hoe Drew fucked with.

The shit she said about him hitting her up last weekend did get under my skin and I felt some type of way about it. But I would never let another bitch demean me and know it impacted me. I was too much of a good strong woman for that. My damn brother would kick my ass if I did anyway. Just like he made us go take care of the bitches that disrespected me and Nya back in the day.

After I took a step away from the table in the direction of the office, I felt a pair of hands on my shoulders trying to pull me back with force. Then all the sudden, there wasn't any hands pulling on my shoulders anymore, and I saw why.

Nya had grabbed the hoe off of me. I watched her throw two punches like she was a female boxer, hitting the hoe in the face. The girl stumbled backwards knocking into our table. Nya did something unexpected. Instead of continuing to throw them hands like I knew she wanted to do, she reached out putting Drew's ex's wrist in a vice grip. Dragging her ass out of the damn restaurant. Similar to how Drew did that fuck nigga last time we were here.

Looking out the window, I saw her give the bitch another shove pushing her further out the damn door. Nya walked back in all calm and collected. I had to give it to her, I was proud of how she handled herself this time. I didn't feel like the hoe was worth a fight either. But that grabbing on me trying to catch me off guard was some sneaky ass shit. She was lucky we didn't jump her for that. That was some real growth on both our parts to be honest.

"Damn, these niggas need to stop fucking with us!" Nya said sounding mad. Like it was Saint's hoe that came up in here.

"I ain't worried 'bout that trick. Drew knows better than to try and play me sis. But I appreciate you having my back."

"Always."

We straightened the table, then went on about our business like nothing happened. The customers went back to eating their food and it was really like the hoe never stepped foot in here. Satan was testing me today. But I wasn't falling for any of it.

Heading over to the office I noticed the door was slightly ajar. I saw the reason why. Juan had his hand on the inside door handle getting ready to leave out. Perfect timing. I was completely over his ass along with that wife of his.

He opened the door the rest of the way, walking past me and brushing against the side of my body. Giving me a creepy ass smile on the way, which only I saw. Ewwweee. That nigga was straight out gross to me. I couldn't stand his weird ass.

I stood in the open doorway, hands on my hips looking at Drew, whose head turned my way. He walked over to me. I didn't wait a second longer, before grabbing his hand and pulling him out of the office with me. At the same time Nya stepped inside.

It was time to show my man how much I missed him. All of the drama that threatened my peace of mind a minute ago was pushed away. Now I only had one single thing on my mind.

"Byyyyyeee." Nya called out all loud.

I kept walking hand in hand with the man I loved, lifting my free hand to wave good-bye to her without looking. I was on a mission right now.

Saint

Meeting with Juan a couple weeks ago didn't do nothing but piss me the hell off. I had begun to trust him more and was starting to fuck with him heavy, but something wasn't sitting right with me. It wasn't anything he said or did. I just had a gut feeling that he had some ulterior motives. I damn sure didn't want his wife around me or my family again either. Nya told me about the fake shit and how she tried to talk down on them.

I was a nigga from the gutta. I still looked at ten dollars like it meant something. I remembered being out on the block trying to make fucking ten dollars at a time. I might have millions put away in banks legally now along with millions in these streets, but nobody could ever say I acted better than the next mothafucka.

I didn't surround myself with niggas or bitches that acted like they were. This hustle wasn't given to me and maybe that was the issue I had with Juan. I knew some mothafuckas who were handed empires and still put in work to maintain that shit. I could respect that. Hell, I could even respect that nigga Ron uptown for the work he put in at least. Even though his ass tried to play me.

He was already paying for that shit too. Both those niggas were dealing with the fall out of how bad they fucked up. New Orleans was becoming mine more and more every day. My lieutenants had put on more niggas adding them to the team on a street level. Some of them even switching up on their old bosses across town. I didn't want rats or bitch niggas working for me. But some of the shit I was hearing made it acceptable.

That nigga Ron was wilding this last month as he saw his sales drop, pockets become light and customers to decline. Not only was he taking that shit hard, the rumor was he was on that shit and fucking up when it came to staying real with his day one niggas.

The same right hand nigga of Ron's that I let take out Smoke back at Calliope had reached out to me wanting to discuss some shit. I was cool on the shit at first, but then Boy confirmed that he was on the outs with Ron and not at his own doing. It turned out Ron tried to play him pussy in front of the whole crew. This nigga was supposed to the mothafucka's day 1 partna, and he kicked his ass out like it was nothing. Telling him to kick rocks with the snap of a fucking finger. I would have never been able to do some shit like that to Buck.

So I was planning to actually let him talk and hear the nigga out. But not right away. I wanted to wait a while to make sure it wasn't some bullshit, trying to bring me down. Not that Ron was capable of that shit single-handedly. Since my plug was one of the heads of CJNG, it was gonna be hard to for these niggas around here to take me out by killing me. But there was still other ways. And after spending six months in a Mexican prison, added to the time I did behind walls years back, I damn sure wasn't trying to do no more time or take another lick. So I would take my time in case I got wind of some other shit going on.

In the meantime, life was good. Shit it was perfect. I felt like I was on top of the world every damn morning when I woke up to Nya next to me and saw my youngin' growing bigger by the day. That was the shit gangsta's didn't deserve. But since I was lucky enough to get I was holding onto that shit. That was why I was driving to the jewelers now. I wasn't just headed this way to pick up some ice to spoil Nya with. It was time I do this shit the right way and make her my wife.

I already knew she was down for me for life. But I wanted her to be protected by my name if I was gone. Shit, I wanted her to be protected by that shit while I was living too. More than that I wanted her to be legally mine. She already was mine anyway. Fuck what you heard. Her mind, body and pussy were on lock already.

As I stepped in Mignon Faget Jewelers I walked around stopping in front of the cherry wood glass case that had an assortment of engagement rings. I saw the top tier where the biggest stones were, deciding on the set I was getting for Nya. It was perfect and the cost didn't mean shit.

When the saleswoman came up and I told her what I wanted, she repeated the price two damn times. I asked her if they took cash and she led me over to the register where there was a money counter behind her. When I laid the stacks of bills out, the woman changed her attitude real fucking quick.

Leaving out of the store, the ring box in my pocket, I felt even more confident that I wanted to do this shit. Nya deserved to be my wife. I didn't even look at these other bitches anymore. She was it for me.

I headed out the entrance of the mall that I entered in through. Then hopped in my whip. Looking in the rear view mirror I noticed a car a few spots over, to the side, with some niggas looking a little too hard at my moves. I reached for my heat, setting it on my lap as I drove off. The niggas didn't follow me, but the shit was suspicious. I was downtown so there was a possibility that it was some of the opposition scoping out my whereabouts.

That was why I wasn't with Nya or Jolie coming out this way for now. Soon enough there wouldn't be no more opposition. But for the time being shit was hot.

I hit the bridge and my thoughts went right back to Nya. Her ass was gonna be surprised as hell when I asked her to marry me. Neither one of us really talked about the future that way. I already called her my wife and she accepted it for what it was. She didn't put any expectations on our relationship. It was all unspoken. We knew how deep this shit went.

Normally, I would have had Jolie plan the party for the proposal. But she was busy as hell with her own shit. Being the mother of two kids. Plus I didn't want her running her mouth and Nya find out.

The shit was going down on Valentine's Day at my strip club. I was turning it into a whole new venue specifically for the night. Anything for my queen. I had missed out on her Birthday this past year since it was while I was locked up in Mexico. Really all our holidays had been fucked up behind some bullshit either going on in the streets or between us. The last time we actually celebrated anything was for my birthday.

That shit was unacceptable. I had to do better.

At least now, with my position more secure in the streets there wasn't anything preventing this shit from popping off. I needed to go over to the club to meet up with the event planner that I hired and see what the hell she was talking about. Valentine's Day was only a few days away and all this was pretty last minute. But with no budget there shouldn't be no problems in pulling out all the stops.

I parked outside the side door, walking up to the building. Then used my key to unlock the place. It was still early as hell in the day and I was the only one here right now. I closed the club down for the entire week, paying all my workers and strippers fat ass bags for the shit. Some of them would work the engagement party. But for the most part, I was doing this shit on the upscale and grown ass man tip.

I turned on the lights and disengaged the security system after the door closed behind me. Looking in front of me I was already impressed with the set up the planner had pulled together. Nya was gonna love the shit and be surprised out of her mind. I went to my office, locked the ring in my safe and waited to finalize the details with the planner when she got here.

Drew

Jolie walked down the hall then made her way over to me. I scooted my chair back from the table as she came closer, standing between my legs. She had on some small ass white silk robe that didn't do shit to cover her thick thighs. Her ass and titties were spilling out. On another morning I would have threw her ass on the table and busted that pussy open.

But today I needed to handle some shit with my mom and then get up with Saint. There was some important shit I wanted to tell him about the uptown crew. This new information would help move things along faster on all fronts.

Saint was trying to piece together a plan as far as taking out Pedro without stepping on his plug's toes. Juan was dragging his damn feet not wanting to fucking help. That meeting yesterday was some straight bullshit. Juan wasn't trying to get his "hands dirty" according to him. His ass didn't want to back Saint without the cartel giving the go ahead.

He was acting like a straight bitch. I could tell Saint wasn't feeling his attitude. That's why I needed to tell him the shit I heard last night. Me and Jolie kicked it for a few hours after leaving the restaurant. After fucking her to sleep all I wanted to do with layup with my bitch and take my ass to sleep with her. But instead, I had to take care of some dumb shit.

I dipped out for a minute going over to this hoe's spot that I used to fuck with. I wasn't on that cheating shit, but this bitch was blowing up my phone saying all types of shit. Talking about she was pregnant and that Jolie threatened her and the baby's life. I didn't know what the hell she was talking about. I hadn't smashed since before I started fucking with Jolie officially.

I cut her off right along with the rest of the hoes as soon as Jolie gave me the pussy and she became my woman. But this bitch had been going around trying to claim me since then apparently. None of the hoes I fucked with except Jolie ever had a spot in my life besides taking the dick from time to time.

After I got to the girl's house and said some real shit to her, letting her know I wasn't the one she wanted problems with, she ended up crying admitting that she was lying. There wasn't a damn baby. Then she went to throwing herself at me trying to take my dick out and drop down to give me head. But all I saw was a desperate bitch. The hoe wasn't even attractive to me anymore. After being with someone like Jolie, none of these women even came close to her. The bitch said any and everything. But I zipped my fucking pants back up and pushed her off me.

I got up to leave, done listening to the damn girl. She already confessed that there wasn't a baby. So there wasn't a point in me being there longer than I had to be. She rushed over to me holding my arm before I made it out the damn door. Running her fucking mouth mentioning the beef between our team and the uptown crew.

I ended up staying long enough to hear what she had to say, but as soon as she said what the fuck I was waiting for, I bounced. There wasn't anything she could say that would make me want to be with her or stick my dick in any of her holes.

Jolie pressed herself up against me and sat on my leg, perched with her hand finding my dick through the pants I had on. I gave her a kiss and rubbed her thigh. Forcing myself to finish the coffee in front of me and not take shit further with her the way I wanted.

"Where are you going?" She asked.

"I gotta stop by my momma's and then handle some shit."

"Oh yeah? When am I meeting your mother? I mean, you're always talking about her. I know how important she is to you, so I would love to meet the woman who's responsible for you becoming the man you are."

"Soon." I kept it short.

I loved Jolie and I loved my mother. But my mom was overprotective. She was a lot to deal with. I wasn't trying to bring Jolie around her anytime soon and fuck up what we had going on. The two would meet more like around the time we were getting married. I had already thought that shit out.

"Mhhhhhmmm" She turned her head, "Okay Drew... And what are you and Saint really up to? Is there more stuff in the streets I should be worried about? I don't need to know everything, but I do understand some things. I mean I was helping run the shit while he was gone. I just want to make sure my family is safe." She asked.

"We got some tension between us and the rest of the city right now. But it's on the way out. I promise as soon as it is, ya'll good to go about your business like you're used to. I'm with Saint on this. I don't want you involved. Just keep holding shit down here."

I gripped her fat ass, filling up my hands with the mothafucka. Then lifted her up gently placing her feet back on the ground in front of me and slapping her ass. Her breathing picked up. Her lust filled eyes let me know she was ready to fuck. Damn, my dick was hard as fuck, ready to go too. I reached down and adjusted it to the side, picking up my phone, wallet and keys off the table, placing them in my pockets. Then backed Jolie up against the dining room table like I had wanted to do.

I slid my hand under her robe, finding her pussy hot and warm, already wet. I stuck two fingers in and watched her Jolie's face tense up while she instinctively bit her bottom lip sexy as fuck. Her pussy walls closing in and juices coating my fingers. She lifted her hand onto my shoulder, enjoying the feelings from my fingers working inside her.

I worked them in and out, going faster using my thumb to press on her hard clit. Just that quick her breathing caught in her chest and her pussy tightened more, putting pressure on my fingers. I slid them up deeper with a curved motion, hitting her fucking Gspot.

Jolie's body shook and she squeezed my shoulder digging her nails into my skin through the shirt. Her cum flowed down while she rotated her hips, soaking my fingers like it was my dick. I wish like fuck it was my dick buried in the mothafucka right now.

I slowly pulled my hand away. Jolie grabbed my wrist with her neatly manicured fingers. My woman was sexy as fuck. She brought my hand to her mouth and licked each finger that I just used to please her with. Tasting her own juices, letting her thick lips wrap around my fingers, enjoying the shit.

"Don't think it's that easy bae. Trying to appease me now, making me wait for what I really want. Your ass is gonna have to wait now."

"Quit playing. You know I'm gonna be all up in that pussy as soon as I get back. That was just something to remember me by while I'm gone." I answered placing a small kiss on her cheek, ready to head out.

"Okkkkayyy Drew!!! We'll see." She smiled at me.

Damn there was that beautiful ass smile, her dimples on the sides of her mouth even turned me on. I wanted to lick and kiss those mothafuckas too.

"Love you girl." I called out opening and closing the front door.

I loved that shit. The being natural and real shit. Being able to touch and fuck my woman whenever and however I wanted.

It only took a little over an hour to get from New Orleans to Baton Rouge, where my mother still lived. She stayed in the same house I grew up in. She kept the small house exactly the way I remember and every time I was in town to visit, it was like I never left.

When I pulled up and saw her car wasn't in the driveway I gave her a call. It was a Friday morning and my mom was like clockwork. She never went out of the house before noon any day of the week. She was always home. She picked up after a few rings, sounding like she was having a good ass time somewhere.

See my mother was a good mother, but she was a straight up alcoholic. She drank from morning to night and would end up passed out on the couch every night of my childhood. She never held a job a day in her life. This house was paid in the clear by her family. But as far as food and other shit, all of it came from the government. That was the main reason I turned to husting when I was a teenager.

I lived in an almost all black part of the city as it was, making me stand out. Not that I gave a fuck about skin color. But being white, coming to school with old clothes, and dingy shit made me a target for mothafuckcas trying to play me for a pussy.

That's how I learned to fight and hold my own. When I was 13 the wrong boy tried to jump me with his friend. I ended up holding my own and beating their asses so damn bad that most mothafuckas' left me alone from that day on.

That's when I decided that this wasn't fucking living. I wanted to be like the dope boys on the corner in my neighborhood. The ones that stayed laced in the flyest shit. All new everything.

I knew some boys around the same age that lived near me, but never hung with any of them. I got up the nerve to ask them how to make some money, and started coming around every day after school. Nobody told me to leave or stay the fuck away. After a month, I convinced them to put me on with the crew they were hustling for. I knew they did that shit more as a joke at first. But I was made for fucking hustlin'.

Any and everything I could flip. But being young and new to the shit, my dumb ass sold to an undercover the second week of selling dime bags. That shit landed me in Juvie. I could have gotten off free and clear and kept a clean record if I snitched on the man supplying me. The police kept asking but I wouldn't say shit. I wouldn't snitch. I knew the rules in the streets.

The rest was fucking history. I did 3 months and when I got out the neighborhood embraced me fully. I had proved myself by taking my lick and keeping my mouth shut.

From that point on, I worked my ass off to come up off the block. Now look at me.

Hearing my mom's voice, I already knew she was on one.

"Hey, ma where you at? I'm at the house?"

"Oh baby, I'm in Atlantic City! Can you believe it?" She answered happily.

"What are you doing in New Jersey?"

"My friend brought me. Wasn't it nice of him?"

"Mom I'll talk to you when you get back."

"Okay I love you Andrew." She said before I ended the call.

I wasn't even mad at my mother. It was the same shit. She was conned by some man selling hear a dream. This shit was nothing new. She just never ran off to places with them when I was younger. She had some damn sense as a mother. She used to have all kinds of men after her when I was growing up. She was tall, beautiful with thick brown straight hair. That was where I got my hair color and complexion from. But now, every time I saw her she just looked older and more tired. I knew it was the effects of the drinking catching up with her. But no matter what she was still my mother.

I hopped in my ride making my way back to New Orleans. Saint was at the club when I called so that's where I was going. He needed to hear this shit sooner rather than later, face to face. We stayed off the fucking phones. Data towers gave up locations and all our business needed to remain off the radar.

I pulled in behind his car and walked over to the side door. Saint was opening the shit before I could knock. He must have been watching the damn cameras. There were some people working on the inside and the place looked completely different than usual. The tables were cleared out with black and white decorations everywhere. It looked like Saint had some kind of special event going on here this weekend.

"This shit looks nice." I told him.

"'Preciate that. It's all for Nya this weekend. I'm proposing and shit." He said nonchalantly.

That was just like his ass, to downplay shit. But he was his own man and that's how he was about everything.

"It's a good look for you. You think she's gonna say yes?" I asked jokingly.

"You know she ain't got a damn choice. She's locked the fuck in already. To mothafuckin' grave. But she deserves all of this... So what's happenin'?" He asked leading the way to his office.

"A bitch I used to fuck with was running her mouth last night, talking 'bout the uptown crew. Seems like ol' boy is really on that shit like we heard. She also mentioned something about a big time Mexican drug dealer coming in town tonight. She's supposed to dance at the party being thrown. The bitch overheard one of Ron's workers mention your name but didn't know shit else." I told him, not leaving anything out.

Saint waited for a minute. I could see the wheels turning in his head. He opened his desk drawer and pulled out one of his phones. The one that he hardly ever used. Mothafuckas' close to him were the only people that even saw the damn thing. Saint was paranoid as fuck, but I couldn't blame him.

I only heard one side of the conversation once whoever was on the line picked up.

"I need the appetizer before dinner." He said calmly into the phone.

To anyone else, it would have seemed to be a simple conversation, but it was code. That was how this higher level shit went. If you had to talk on a phone, you didn't say shit.

"Give my thanks. I'll wait for dessert." Shit I wasn't even a hundred percent on what

225

the hell he was talking about. But I knew it had to do with what I just told him.

Saint turned his attention back to me. The fact that he even conducted the phone call with me in his office said a lot about our partnership. He was like me in a lot of ways, not trusting mothafuckas. That was how you had to be in the game. Say as little as possible and work your ass off to make shit happen. Always stay ten steps ahead. There were rules to this shit.

"We're good to take Pedro out tonight. You got a location for the party. I want to make it clean and smooth. No fuck ups. It's just gonna be a couple of us in on this shit."

"It can only be at a few spots. I know it's uptown. That's where the girl's from. I can get the location from her. Are we taking out the competition too?" I asked wondering if he wanted to take this opportunity to get rid of Ron and Marlo while we had the chance. It would make things easier for him in the city.

"Nah. We'll wait. If you kill a nigga there's ten more on some payback shit. I'm gonna let them mothafucka's deal with the consequences of breaking an agreement with me. Then if they can't handle the shit like real ass men, I'll go that route. Pedro is the man we're after tonight. Go ahead and get up with that girl and give me the drop when you get it."

"Already."

"Aye, I'm not trying to be in your shit. But if you fuck over my sister, you fuck me over, ya' heard meh." He flat out said.

"I know. She's good." I answered. Shit, I did know that before I even got with Jolie. Even though I was with a bitch last night it wasn't what it looked like. But I was a man myself first and didn't answer to nobody breathing. I wasn't about to explain my moves to Saint, even if he was technically my boss. "How you gonna get at him in the party. There's gonna be heavy ass security?" I asked wondering what his plan was. I knew he had shit figured out that was how he worked. Methodical and smart.

"I got someone in mind to handle him. Get me that shit, and any other information you can, then we'll meet up before going up there."

I nodded my head, slapped hands with him from across the desk as I stood and headed back out. Damn, now I had to delay getting back to Jolie longer. I had to go deal with this same hoe. Strictly on business, but still. Jolie would just have to understand. Or never find out.

Nya

As soon as Saint walked in the bedroom, I knew he was there. Without turning around, seeing or hearing him I felt his presence.

I spoke out to him, "Hey bae, what are you doing back so early?"

"I need to talk to you." He responded.

I knew he was about to say some serious shit. His tone was off. So real quick I mentally prepared myself for whatever it was. It didn't sound good whatever he was about to lay on me.

I sat down on the side of the bed, resting my hand on the Kwamir's back. I had just fed and changed him before laying him down in the middle of the bed to take a nap. He really was a go good baby for being only a few months old. He went to sleep easily most of the time and as long as he was fed and hardly cried.

"Wassup?" I asked.

Saint walked over. He required my full undivided attention standing in front of me, looking at me ominously. The look he was giving me, was the same one that most niggas feared. But I wasn't most niggas and I didn't fear his ass. To me this look meant something different. He was worried about

228

something and hesitating. That shit wasn't like him at all.

"We got the go ahead to take Pedro out. I'm waiting for his location now. But it can only be handled by a bitch."

My ears perked up. Was he asking me to be involved in this? I was more than ready to ride for my man.

"The thing is, it's gonna be all you baby. You gotta act like a stripper to get the job done. I really ain't feeling it. But I can't trust nobody else but you on this. I know how lethal your ass is and it's gonna take that same shit I seen in you before."

I didn't hesitate, "You already know I'm with the shit. What do I need to do, just say the word bae?"

I stood up wrapping my arms around his neck coming up on my tiptoes to get closer to his defined lips. Giving him a long sensual kiss.

"I don't like this shit shawty. But I know you can handle it. If anything goes wrong, I won't be able to get to you right away. I'm gonna be posted outside with Drew the whole time." He ignored my kiss and pulled back.

I continued kissing on him from his cheeks, down his neck and his collarbone. All over his beautiful brown skin.

"You know how serious this is NyAsia?" He grabbed my arms and forced me back. "We're talking cartel shit, not some bum ass nigga off the street. It's gonna be a team of mothafucka's watching him all night, surrounding him. You got to be on your shit a hundred percent to get him alone and take him out without drawing attention to yourself. Chill out for a minute and listen, ya heard meh!" He literally backed up himself now.

Ah, hell no. Now I was fuming. I understood all the shit he was saying was important, but damn if it was about to get real tonight and I was gonna be in danger, than I damn sure wanted some dick now. That way my head wasn't fucked up later, or in case it was the last time. Not that I was gonna mention that to Saint. I didn't want him to think I wasn't capable of doing what he was asked. I was.

I would listen to whatever plan he had come up with, go in the place, take the mothafucka out and then make it out of there no problem. Back to my family. But all that shit could happen after my nigga made love to me. I needed to feel his love before I took on this challenge.

I folded my arms over my chest, and tapped my foot, showing him how I was feeling from his rejection.

"Okay, Saint! I get it. But that don't change that we're here now and I want you to make love to me first. After you make me cum, I'll sit down and listen to whatever you want, *daddy*." I said getting more into what I was saying.

I couldn't help it that my nigga turned me on the way he did. Hell, he did this shit to me. Dickmatizing me the way he did from the very beginning.

He scooped my ass up and walked over to the on-suite master bathroom. Yesss! I was getting my way. I knew he couldn't resist me. Plus that damn bulge in his pants wasn't fooling nobody.

He closed the door behind him, since Kwamir was in our room sleeping. And set me down on my feet in front of the double sink countertop. I wasted no time undressing taking my shirt and pants off in record time. Saint did the same. Watching each other until we both stood naked.

My eyes were drawn to his tattoos. I swear my pussy got wetter as my eyes went lower seeing his dick standing at attention, knowing how he was about to make me feel.

He came over to me and roughly turned me around, "arch your back, get that ass up." He instructed me. I obediently came on my tiptoes and leaned over placing my hands closer to the wall side of the granite counter.

The coolness of the stone on my already hot body, made every place he was touching more sensitive without him trying to.

He didn't waste any more time, before gripping my ass cheeks apart and sliding all 10 inches in nice and slow. That shit caused me to come up on my toes more, leaning over farther trying to adjust. "Ahhhh, baby. That shit feels so good."

I started bouncing my ass, slowly at first, then rotating my hips loving his big ass dick hitting all sides of my walls.

"You playing with me now."

He lowered himself making his dick come up with every stroke. That shit had me coming up almost off my feet while he picked up the pace. Reaching around, he found my breasts and rolled my sensitive nipples between his fingers. Then he pinched down on them before changing his grip and moving his hands to my waist. Taking control of my body as we moved in sync. I continued to work my pussy on him throwing it back as hard as I could.

He had me locked in, not able to move anything except my pussy back on him. The shit hurt and felt good as hell, the pressure built up in me from my core radiating down to my pussy. He really fucked me up when he took deeper strokes going into my damn kidneys or some shit.

I stopped altogether like he always caused me to do. It was too much, too big, too damn everything. I clenched down my pussy muscles. Cum gushed out covering Saint's dick, dripping down my thighs.

Saint took that as his cue to go back to work and fuck up my insides some more.

"Baby." I whined.

"Look at this shit. Take the mothafuckin' dick Nya." I looked up into the mirror in front of me and saw exactly what he wanted me to see.

He slowed down again, and I arched my back more. Watching our bodies come in contact with every stroke. My ass jiggling and him gripping my ass. Then he slapped the bitch and I was forced to look down again, from seeing fucking stars and shit from the intense pain he caused with his last few strokes. I screamed out, "Ahhhhhhh!!!!" while I cummed again this time with him buried in me.

He pushed me further onto the counter so my feet were all the way off the floor, body scrunched up and twisted from the shit.

Saint's dick game was something else. But that was the first time the shit caused me to almost black out. I had learned to take it any and every way, but the intensity of what he made me feel really sent me over the edge. It was the strongest feelings and orgasm I ever had.

The sex with him just kept getting better. This nigga could have my body and mind any way he wanted. It was all his. God truly blessed him with that thing between his legs. And that wasn't even considering how he used that mouth.

He lifted me up, knowing I couldn't walk at all and sat me on the edge of our full size double Jacuzzi tub. He ran the water checking for the right temperature. After putting in my favorite peach scent bath balls, he picked me up again and eased me down into the warm water.

"You know my walk's gonna be fucked up now right?" I joked.

"You gonna have to suck that shit up for tonight shawty. There can't be no weak bitches on my team." He teased.

I knew he was still tense about letting me do the job tonight. This was our chance to get rid of Pedro and the last of his true enemies once and for all. There were still a few minor players that had limited time on this earth. But after Pedro was gone we both could sleep easier at night.

"I promise I'll listen and do everything you say for real. I know how important this is."

Saint leaned over the edge, then walked out the bathroom. I watched him go over to the bed and rub Kwamir's back before walking out of the room. I already knew where I would find him when I finished. He was gonna be right up in the room he designated as his office downstairs. When Saint's mind was on business or the streets that was all he could think about until whatever it was settled.

Pedro blindsiding him, then having him sent to that Mexican Prison was that other level shit cartels could pull. That was what he was talking about when he made sure to tell me how serious this shit was repeatedly. I understood all that. But there was no way I would give this responsibility to any other woman. We were the ones that had the most to lose or gain. I would do anything for my family.

I went ahead and laid back, grabbed my loofa and began rubbing the body wash all over my skin. Taking time to let my pussy soak and recuperate. Tonight I was gonna be a stripper *again.*

I finished getting ready, and stood in the full length mirror in the corner of our room admiring my reflection and taking time to look over everything in detail. I needed to play my part well. According to Saint, Pedro would have no less than 3 security guards near him tonight at all times. It was my job to get a cue from a nigga Saint had on the inside to lead him off into one of the private rooms, and then when he least expected take him out.

I wouldn't have any weapons on me other than two blades I was keeping. Both placed strategically in my braids that I was leaving half up in a high bun on top. One tucked away in each side.

The blades were my bigger ones. But nothing over an inch and a half. They were sharp and ready to do the job. One of these blades could slice through flesh easily. But there were only a few places I could cut that would fulfill the requirement. Either his neck, wrists, or behind the knee would be my only options. The neck was the best bet because it led to death faster. Not a lot of mothafuckas took blades serious, but I learned early on that they were the damn truth.

Saint came in and stood behind me in the mirror. I was wearing a one piece bodysuit of sorts. It was actually one of the pieces of lingerie me and Jolie had ended up buying after having the babies, to motivate us to get our bodies back. I was lucky in that my body being on the slim thick side naturally snapped back in the first month. She still had a little extra baby weight left, but she was still bad as hell. Just thicker in all the right places, if you asked me.

The bodysuit was gold with a sequenced pattern and sheer in between giving a see through effect all over. The back came up into a thong, accentuating my round ass cheeks and making them look even bigger from how it hit my curves. I chose to wear my highest pair of heels even though they didn't match. They were a pair of strappy black platform heels that I would never have worn out of the damn bedroom if it wasn't for tonight.

I probably should have felt nervous, but I wasn't at all. Not that I considered myself a real ass stripper for my one night only half way doing the shit. But I knew my role, knew what needed to be done and that was that. I could handle whatever was thrown at me, was my attitude.

Saint was all business too. Normally if he saw me in a fit like this he would have lost his damn mind and dropped some more dick in my life. But instead, he kept distance and nodded his head in approval. I went to the closet and grabbed my full length wool coat. It wasn't as expensive as my fur one, but that would draw too much attention. I needed to look like the baddest bitch in the place, but I also needed to play my part and not set off any red flags.

My makeup was completely different than usual. I hoped that the club was dark enough that when I made my entrance nobody recognized me. Mothafuckas around the city knew me. That was why I was entering well after the party started, and coming in the back to find my target. To get him by myself I would keep my head low and look for the perfect opportunity.

"If someone recognizes you, get out of there. We're gonna be right out back the whole time for when you leave out. Same spot we're dropping you off at."

"I know."

"If you don't see any opportunity just leave out without trying some shit that will get you caught up."

"I know.

"If some shit don't seem..."

"I know bae. I got this. If something is off, I'm out of there. You ain't gotta worry."

"I ain't gotta worry and my fucking heart is in the hands of a room full of niggas. I don't even wanna let you up outa of this house shawty."

"I love you too." I replied simply.

He brushed his hand over his hair in a downward motion. Yeah, his ass was on edge. We had gone through the different scenarios over and over. It was time to make this shit happen.

After walking down the stairs I went over to Jolie holding Joy and gave her a light hug. Then made my way to the swing and stopped it long enough to give Kwamir a kiss goodbye while BJ was laid out beside Jolie on the couch for the night. She was here to stay while we were gone.

"Love ya sis." I said.

"Love you girl."

Drew said his good-bye to Jolie and we headed out. On the ride downtown me and Saint didn't say a thing to each other. It was a tense ass ride other than the blunt Drew was smoking and music playing. I was in my head focused with my hand clasped inside of Saint's strong one resting on his knee.

It was 3 in the morning when we pulled into the parking lot of Scores. This was the local strip club in the quarter that people form here usually went to. I was kind of surprised that Ron and Marlo would have had this shit here. But that was on them.

When saint did shit, he did the shit. Not halfway or trying to be on the cheaper end. According to Saint, this man Pedro was into submissive black girls. That was why his ass was coming to a spot like this when he had enough paper to do shit big himself. It was just like some Mexican mothafucka to think he was in charge and above us "blacks" in the streets but be turned on by some black pussy. That shit was about to cost the mothafucka his life.

Saint squeezed my thigh and gave me a light kiss, before I opened the back door to Drew's Range. Walking up to the back of the building I spotted some nigga waiting outside by himself, just like Saint told me there would be. When I made it to the door, he pulled back on the door handle that I realized he had been keeping from closing all the way. Then inconspicuously closed it right behind me after I walked inside the dark hallway of the club.

Once inside, the man nodded his head the side in the direction straight in front of me. I stared down the dimly lit hall taking in my surroundings. There was a clear view of the table in VIP that Pedro was seated at. The man who let me in stayed put by the door, while I walked down. Trying to keep in the shadows on the side as much as possible.

I slowed my pace for a moment, letting my coat fall to the floor, before anyone saw me do the shit. No one could know I just randomly showed up. I had to make it look like I was just another stripper in attendance like all the other ones I saw out on stage and by the tables now that I was closer.

Taking a few more steps getting closer to my target. Another stripper walked down the hall passing me with a big ass smile on her face, "bitch you better get in there! Get your money up. They're throwing that shit around now that they're drunk!"

I played it off, acting the part, "Yessss hunny" I smiled wide back. I would have given her an ass a high five really getting in the role, but her hands were full of the bills she just earned.

I kept walking, focused only on the reason I was here. I stayed back in the cut near where the hallway opened up into the main floor. Scoping shit out and seeing what I was really dealing with.

In front of me was the VIP spot Pedro was seated in with some of his men. The VIP sections in the club sat up higher than the other tables that were spread out a few feet off the long stage. These exclusive tables were up close, front and center to the main stage. Like all strip clubs the lights were low with spotlights shining on the dancer on stage.

Around the floor there were at least a dozen strippers dancing around the room, most up in the VIP sections where the most money could be made. I saw Marlo and Ron sitting across from where I stood, at another VIP section, on the other side of the stage with their niggas around them. That shit was perfect for what I had planned.

Pedro was sitting back alone, with one security guard behind him. He was focused on one of the thick dark skin strippers in front of him. She was bent over, hands on the floor touching her toes, shaking her ass to the beat of the song playing.

It was now or never.

Another stripper came out on stage after being announced. "Taste" by Tyga and Offset thumped through the speakers. Making all the strippers in the place to go to work popping their pussies on niggas.

I took the final steps over to Pedro's chair and leaned down, slowly bringing my hands across the back of the leather chair he was in as seductively as possible. Every move I made was calculated with one purpose in mind.

"Hey, Papi."

He barely looked up in acknowledgement, his eyes now glued to the bitch on stage working the pole upside down.

Damn, I had to do something more to get his attention and use what I knew about him to my advantage. But at least he didn't dismiss me altogether.

I moved my body, slowly winding my hips in a seductive way, in front of him. Taking a risk and sliding my hands from his shoulders down his torso. I rested them on his chest then made eye contact. He was looking at me now.

Fuck it. It was time to go all in. I squatted down legs gapped, shoulders back, not breaking eye contact. Then brought both my hands down lowering them slowly from his chest. Applying slight pressure with my nails, going lower. Down to his thighs and stopping close to his dick. Finally breaking eye contact and letting my eyes follow my hands and look at his crotch, before I looked back up.

Pedro's eyes were heavy from either the alcohol or weed. In a room full of naked women and loud music I now had his full attention. His eyes were locked on me alone, filled with lust. I had his ass.

"I just want to *please* you, papi! Anything you want." I said in a higher than normal voice.

Sweetly and passively, showing his dominance over me. Then I boldly moved both hands directly over his dick, rubbing against the bulge in his pants. I cringed inside, but kept my composure as his small nasty dick grew harder under my touch. I had to do this shit no matter how disgusted I was by the man in front of me.

"Get your ass up." He snapped in his heavy accent.

I stood up right away, and looked down at him sheepishly, thinking I had fucked up. Instead he reached out, cupped my pussy through the see-through fabric and then brought it back to his nose, checking my scent.

"Perro culo negro." He said.

I had no clue what that shit meant. But I continued to look at him, head bowed, until he stood up and grabbed me by the hand roughly. He turned and walked to the side of the section where there was a small ramp leading to a curtained room.

His security guard that was standing a few feet behind him followed us to the room. Pedro led me inside and once in the room, his security stood at the entrance, pulling the curtain closed. Leaving me and Pedro alone while he stood outside keeping watch. It was obvious this wasn't the first time Pedro had brought a girl back here. Hell, none of that mattered to me. I had one more goal to accomplish. I just didn't know how I was gonna make that shit happen when there was his security standing a few feet away with a team of other mothafuckas for protection. But I would find a way.

Pedro let go of my hand and sat own on the oversized, high-back curved ottoman. Everything in the room was made to look more expensive than it was with a red and black theme. The lights were low, with one main spotlight shining down on a short glass table meant for strippers.

I strutted over to the table, winding my hips again slowly. Then turned around and bent over hands gripping the glass for support, shaking my ass. Pedro's hands came up and squeezed my ass cheeks hard. He started running his hands all over my body. Finding his way to the front, he grabbed my breasts hard and pulled me back into his lap.

I sat on his lap backwards, continuing to listen to music and wait for the perfect time to pull out my razors. Now grinding on his small dick that was hard beneath the fabric of his pants.

"Take off your clothes." He commanded.

I reached up and undid the straps on my shoulders, pulling them down over my arms, so my breasts were fully exposed. I stood up, getting off his lap, turning around. Letting him have full view of what he wanted to see.

I moved back into position, straddling him. My thighs gapped open breasts close to his face, and leaned forward running my fingers through his balding hair. Pedro began to suck on my nipples switching between them both before using his hands to pull my jumpsuit down more. I pretended to enjoy the feelings of him on my body. Moving my hips faster rubbing my pussy against his dick through the material.

I effortlessly freed my razor with my right hand without him noticing and brought it down in one smooth stroke hard against his neck the same way I did to Jaquan. He instantly reached up in panic to grab me, but he was already losing too much blood. He couldn't make a noise or hardly move. I jumped back quietly so his security wouldn't be alarmed. I watched his breathing slow and hands fall to his sides as his eyes locked on the tattoo that was now exposed above my pussy. Clear as day he saw my niggas' name tatted in ink.

Now he knew who sent me. That little bit of satisfaction, made me smile. He knew Saint won. I hurriedly pulled my top back up. I had to come up with some shit quick to get the fuck out of here. Then it hit me.

I reached in Pedro's pants pockets and found what I was looking for. He had a zippo liter and cigar in one of them, so I walked over to the furthest side of the curtain. Away from the end we walked in on and lit the bitch on fire. As it caught fire, I went over to opposite side where we had entered in through. The man who had a gun and could pull out and shoot my ass in a heartbeat stood not even a foot away, on the other side.

I kept my feet back to the side, where he couldn't see them under the curtain. It was only a matter of time now.

In the next minute or two, smoke and the fire drew his attention briefly to the other side of the curtain which must have been a good 10 feet away. I watched his feet moving and as soon as he was getting close to where he could see the actual fire, I ran out of the bitch like the fucking wind. Straight out, bare foot, heels left behind in the room along with a very dead Pedro.

I ran for my life down the hall to the back entrance. Not looking back. The nigga who let me in opened the door and ran out behind me.

Both of us hopped in the Jeep that was waiting for us with the doors open. As soon as my ass touched the damn seat, Drew sped off. Saint sat in the passenger seat not looking back in my direction.

The job was done.

As we pulled out of the parking lot, some mothafucka's ran out of the building and let of rounds but we were already turning the corner. Too far away. None of their bullets making contact.

Ron

Pulling into my pops driveway was the last thing I wanted to be doing. But I was out of fucking options. Saint pulled out the fucking rug from up under us. In the next few weeks my crew would be completely out of business.

I hadn't even come around my family for the past couple of Sunday dinners that my momma had, trying to avoid facing the shit. My pops would want to talk about how shit was going in the streets and I couldn't look him in the eyes and tell him we were about to lose it all.

Unlike Marlo or Saint, I was handed the key to my family organization in the streets that my fucking grandfather had built up. As well as the legit family business of manufacturing I was left to run. We were the oldest family street organization still standing in New Orleans. And from the looks of it, I was on the verge of losing it all

That was why I had started popping pills and drinking more lean lately. Before all this, the only shit I fucked with was liquor and weed. I knew I was wildin' out, but this last deal with Pedro was supposed to solve all our problems and get rid of that fuck nigga "Saint". But the nigga somehow found a way to fuck that shit up too.

At first all three of our crews in the city were cool. Looking back, I regretted ever helping that pussy ass nigga Saint. If I hadn't looked out on that Smoke hit, his ass wouldn't be in the fucking picture. Now he came back from the dead, feeling some type of way about business behind his bitch. But seemed to forget that I was the same nigga who helped him get his shit back when I didn't have to.

His fucking feelings were what caused him to flood the streets with his shit. Like a bitch. The mothafucka knew neither of us from Downtown or Uptown could compete with the shit. If that wasn't bad enough, Pedro couldn't do shit either because Saint was backed by a more powerful cartel and the shit would come back on him.

Last night before he was killed, we had just agreed on a new plan to take back the city and get rid of Saint for good. We were gonna draw his attention away to Houston, while putting the hit on him out there. That would take away the suspicion of it being some local shit connected to Pedro or us.

Everything was good, or supposed to be. That is until fucking NyAsia.

Of all people she was the one who took out the damn plug. The way Saint sent a bitch to do his dirty work was fucked up. What kind of real ass nigga lets his bitch take that kind of risk? Nya wasn't even supposed to be in the streets. She should be sitting at home taking care of her kids, like my mom and her own mother was when she was a kid.

I slammed my fists against the steering wheel and took one final sip from my double cup, setting it back down in the center council. Then got out of the car, unintentionally slamming the door to my black Benz shut. That's how wound up and ready to fucking go that nigga had me.

It was still early as hell. I was coming straight from the strip club, being up all night and dealing with the bullshit after Pedro's body was found. Afterwards I met up with Marlo trying to figure some shit out. But it was useless. Now I was frustrated as hell and still came up with nothing.

This was my last ditch attempt. At this point I didn't even have my day 1 nigga by my side, since he tried to make some comment about calling a truce with Saint. My best friend since childhood trying to tell me what to do set me off, especially taking up for that nigga. I demoted his ass real quick back to street level. His ass would have to learn some loyalty and respect. Shit that I shouldn't have even had to question since we were boys since fucking playground days.

The sun shined down bright as hell like it was a perfect fucking morning, as I slowly walked up to the front door. Already 10 o'clock in the morning. I knew I looked like hell but there wasn't time to go home. I hoped my pops could help do something to make this shit stop. In order to ensure our organization didn't collapse I had to put my pride aside and bring this to him.

He had schooled me on the best and worst of times in the streets under his control, but nowhere did he tell me about a time he almost lost what his father had worked for. I felt like a fucking failure. Back in his day, he was certified and would have never let another nigga one up him, the way Saint was fucking with me.

I knocked on the door and opened it myself, announcing my arrival. My younger sister who was 23 still lived at home since she was going to college and a spoiled ass daddy's girl. She was in the kitchen when I walked up eating some pancakes, eggs with bacon. The shit smelled good as hell, but I didn't have an appetite since my stomach was full from the lean.

My mother turned around, noticing me first. She dropped her spatula on the counter and came over fussing, "What is it baby? What in the hell happened to you?... RONALD!!!!!" She hollered out for my father.

I was a fucking third generation, named after my father and his father. This shit was in my blood. My pops came in the room, and immediately gave me a look. He knew some shit was up.

"Son, come in my office."

"Now, don't go getting mad hunny. He's your son." My momma tried to take up for me.

Neither one of them knew how bad shit was, or so I thought. But she knew my damn father well enough to know his crazy ass looks. When I was a kid and he had that same expression on his face I got my ass whooped. I'm not talking that regular ass beating a kid gets. From the age of about 10 on, I got my ass beat like I was a grown ass man and treated like one in all the ways. That was when he really started hands on grooming for me to take over the same way his father did him.

I followed being my pops, his newspaper folded under his arm and his solid ass walk. This is the nigga I respected and feared more than anyone else alive. Matter of fact, he was the only nigga alive I did. Saint might have thought I was a pussy, but that nigga didn't put fear in my heart. If death called my name so be it.

Once inside the office I went ahead and took a seat across from my father's cherry wood desk. Similar to the shit I had in my office.

"What the fuck happened?" He wasted no time.

"Mane, I don't even know how shit got this bad. But that nigga Saint's 'bout to put us out of business. He flooded the streets with some shit we can't compete with and last night took out our plug. He's protected by the CFNJ, so we can't touch him without it coming back on us. Shit's fucked up pops. I don't know what the fuck to do." I said looking at him, being met with ice cold eyes already scolding me.

"You bring this shit to me now? You didn't think to come to me before it got to this point? I put your ass in charge because I thought you had it in you to act like a gotdamn boss! Not a fucking pussy. You let this nigga take what's OURS, and you sitting here high as a fucking kite. You're unfit to even sit in that mothafuckin' chair right now nigga."

I hung my head, arms and hands resting on the side of the chair. I took a deep swallow, "I'm sorry. I know I fucked up."

He nodded his head in agreement. "I knew some shit was wrong. I heard some shit, but didn't wanna believe my own son was fucking up this bad."

"Is there anything we can do?" I asked.

"You mean is there anything I can do, to save your ass... Does this nigga Saint have any family in the city?"

I knew what he was getting at. When mothafuckas went to war like this we could use someone in their family as collateral. Honestly this shit happened so fast, I hadn't even considered it as an option. My head had been fucked up and judgment clouded.

"He got a sister and... you remember NyAsia" His eyes lit up. "Well, she's *his* bitch. They got a fucking baby and everything now." I said hearing the disdain in my own voice.

Thinking about her opening her fucking legs for that nigga left me with a bad taste in my mouth. I hadn't even been good enough to see what the pussy was hitting for when we used to kick it back in the day.

My pops didn't say anything for a few minutes just nodded his head, running his hands over his beard in deep thought. "It's some shit you don't know. But it might be the thing to get this nigga off our backs for good. In the meantime, sure up the blocks and get off that shit. I'm telling you now son, I'm back in charge until you get your shit together. Ain't no mothafuckin' way we're losing 3 generations of work because you wasn't fucking thinking. I'll have more product by the end of the week and that shit will be quality. Make sure the team is ready."

"What about Saint? He ain't going nowhere."

"He aint?" My pops said as a question, not giving an answer. At this point I felt like a failure but my pride didn't mean shit when it came to our operation.

"Now go eat your mothers' fucking food and you betta not so much as look the wrong fucking way to make her think something's wrong with you. The last thing she needs is to be worrying about your ass."

He ended the conversation and motioned his hand for me to leave. Dismissing me the same way he did when I was a child. I felt like a fucking kid again. But at least Saint would finally get what was coming to him. When my pops said some shit, he made that shit happen. I had never seen him not follow through. He was as thorough as they came.

Saint

My bitch having that mothafucka's scent on her when we got back to our crib made me wanna go kill his ass all over again. After Jolie left and we checked on the baby in his room, I sat her down. I didn't even give her a chance to wash up and take a shower before I interrogated her. I wanted to hear every fucking detail, with her leaving nothing out. My mind wouldn't stop wondering how far shit went and how she handled herself without me there, until she told me every fucking thing.

"He was already drunk. It wasn't nothing to get him to go with me to the room. Then I started dancing and took my razor out. I got out of there by setting the curtain on fire, drawing his guard away so I could run out."

"I don't wanna hear that bullshit! Tell me everything."

"Saint... it's done. I killed the man, it's over."

"Nah baby, I need to know all the shit you not telling me."

"Why?" She got loud. Seeing I wasn't budging she began rattling everything that happened in detail.

"He rubbed on my body, touched my breasts, put his mouth on me, saw my tattoo, then I ended the shit." She ended up revealing.

After she told me everything I sat down on the bed next to her and took my time thinking shit over. I was fucking seeing red knowing that another man touched her. I knew I sent her in there. I knew I put her at risk. Maybe that was what was fucking with me the most. Maybe I wasn't worthy of Nya.

The only relief came knowing Pedro was no longer breathing and that he saw my name tatted above her pussy. That shit was what was keeping me from losing fucking control altogether.

A part of me felt like I should have never put my bitch in danger like I did or let another man get close knowing he was gonna be touching her. I mean what kind of nigga was I to say I had her and was her fucking protector, then send her in? Knowing she's been raped, knowing shit could have went sideways in a fucking blink of an eye. I felt guilty as hell no matter how many times she tried to sugar coat shit or reassure me she wanted to do it and was glad I trusted her to carry this shit out.

Without saying shit else, I took her in the shower and washed her from head to toe not missing a damn spot of her skin. Rubbing away all the remnants of the mothafucka touching her or his smell. Then I made love to her. The shit I only did when I was in my fucking feelings about shit. The other side to me, that only Nya brought out.

Today was Saturday and with the cloud of the shit that happened last night hanging over our heads it almost made me cancel my plans to propose tonight. I was sitting with Kwamir feeding him on the couch with Sports Center on relaxing in some baller shorts and a wife beater. This was the shit I looked forward when to I was home. The peace my family brought me. But even now, my mind kept going back to last night.

The doorbell rang. Right on time. It was exactly 12:00. I called out, "Bae, can you get the door? I'm feeding the baby."

Nya walked out from the back laundry room and headed to the door wearing some simple leggings and a t-shirt, still looking good as fuck. Damn I was lucky as hell, just watching her walk around the house made me feel like a king. Fuck my feelings, she deserved every fucking thing. Everything was for her today.

"Ohhhh, baby!" She came into the living room, reaching down from behind me over the back of the couch and wrapping her arms around my shoulders, kissing my neck.

"Thank you. I love all of it." She said excitedly before standing back up and bringing the bouquet of flowers and gift bags over to the table. She had no idea how much more shit was in store for her today. Everything was hers all damn day.

She might have thought I didn't even remember it was Valentines' day, because I had intentionally not said shit about it all week even when she dropped hints or mentioned it. I played the shit off on purpose. I loved my bitch even more for the fact she wasn't with me for a damn thing other than me. Even if she wanted something for Valentine's Day, she would never complain or be mad behind material shit. She was content with whatever. She was a rider through thick and thin. That shit most niggas like me would never find. And I damn sure was holding on to her ass, especially after this shit was official.

I continued to watch her open the card first, reading it out loud being extra. But she could have that shit. "Oh my GAWD! Nigga how did you know?" She asked seriously when she looked in the first bag.

It was two tickets to an opera coming up in 2 months. I had gone on her laptop and looked up everything she was searching in the history. She had searched that shit over and over. Nya always acted hard and the streets had made her heartless with certain shit. But the Nya she was before her parent's death was really soft as hell. She was well

259

taken care of, even spoiled as a kid. She was smart as hell and liked shit like art and operas, that ordinary bitches never even thought of. That's why her ass was cut out to be a fucking lawyer. She was well rounded.

Then she opened the next gift. It was a long rectangular box with a red bow tied on front. She lifted the lid and saw a complete black dress with some silver in the shit. I didn't' pick it out. I actually tricked Jolie into doing the shit one day when I randomly showed her some shit in a magazine and asked what Nya would like. I was real slick about keeping this shit a secret. And pulled it all off in only a couple of weeks.

Towards the bottom of the dress there was a card, with a handwritten invitation from me for tonight.

Mr. Kwame Harris requests the presence of Ms. NyAsia Miller promptly at 9:00 pm
this 14th day of February.

She looked up like a little ass girl on Christmas. This was what I did it for. To see her accepting the love I had for her was real. Making her my fucking queen.

We spent the rest of the day chilling, after I told her that Terrell was gonna watch the baby. She relaxed some since she felt like we couldn't leave him with anyone outside of family and last night he was with Jolie already. She refused to put that on my sister on Valentine's Day.

Little did she know Terrell was bringing Kwamir to the engagement party with him to surprise her ass too. I wanted everybody to be there that she loved to make the shit memorable. Knowing she would want it that way.

Now all we had to do was kick it until tonight came, then get ready. This shit was really about to happen. I probably should have been nervous or some shit. But there wasn't a nervous bone in my body. Nya was already my wife, now it was time to do shit the right way and put it in ink.

Jolie

Saint had told me the other day he wanted me and Drew to meet him at the strip club and then head out to dinner after. The shit probably had something to do with last night, but either way I wasn't letting it fuck up mine and Drew's first Valentine's Day together.

Drew really showed the hell out last night in the bedroom and now I was sore, trying to fix Joy a bottle, having to ease myself down into the rocker in her room, next to her crib. She was just starting to sleep in her crib. Since the first couple of months I kept her in bed with me. But now, there was too much shit me and my man were trying to do in there. She was easy going anyway and adjusted to the change fine. Otherwise, I'm sure me and Drew would have had to just be creative with our fucking and that wasn't a problem either.

BJ was sitting on the floor playing with his tablet, watching the thing intently trying to figure out one of the educational games I had downloaded for him. He was smart as hell, and now being with me he was flourishing. I just needed to keep his dead beat ass mother away especially now that she had that bum ass nigga in her life.

Saint asked me about how I knew him in more detail. When I explained the situation further he was ready to get rid of his ass. I told him to hold off and wait. Right now, I didn't want any unnecessary heat my brother's way.

This shit was my problem for now, if it came to it I promised I would tell him and Drew about it. There was no way Domonique or her nigga really had the best interest of BJ at heart and came at me the way they did. They had some shit up their sleeve and until I figured out what it was I had my guard up. I truly did hope one day his mother would get her shit together and be a part of his life, even as a once in a while situation. To be honest, I wasn't gonna let him go back and live with her at this point. He was my son the same way Joy was my daughter.

Drew must have woke up from Joy's crying like I did. He came meandering into her room standing in the doorway. Wearing a pair of grey sweat pants and a black wife beater, showing off his toned arms and that damn bulge in his pants. Shit like this should be illegal for men to wear. The dick prints in these things were official as hell.

He noticed where my eyes had wondered down and smirked back at my ass cockily. He knew what the fuck was up.

"Stop looking if you aint' ready for it."

"I'm gonna say that same shit to you later. Wait for it."

"Ma J, I'm ready for it. I'm hungry!"

BJ intervened in the adult conversation talking about wanting breakfast. Not understanding the true meaning to what we were talking about. Thank God. Drew and me both busted out laughing, and BJ's smart little ass sat there looking mad like his daddy used to do.

"I'm for real." He hollered to get our attention and try and make the situation as serious as he was. For a four year old he didn't play especially when it came to his food.

"Come on then" I stood up, Joy in my arms still feeding her.

Reaching my other hand down and resting it on BJ's shoulder to reassure him. He snuggled up against the side of my leg. The best feeling in the world were moments like these with my kids. Now that Drew was here to share it with me, it felt even more right. He could have shied away or backed off when he knew I was pregnant knowing the responsibility he would have to take on with me being a single mother. Or really shot up the deuces when I took on BJ full time as my own son. Him standing by my side and acting like it didn't matter that I had a child was one thing. But now, him here being a part of it and stepping up when he didn't have to, was one of the reasons I loved him.

Drew reached out and took Joy from my arms after I crossed through the threshold of the door. He was the only father figure she would know. That shit used to bring tears to my eyes, but now I felt comfortable with it and confident that I made the right decision to let go and let life happen.

After fixing a bowl of cereal for BJ and some cut up apple slices on the side, Drew set Joy down in her swing and came over to where I was sitting on the stool across from BJ. He kissed my cheek leaning forward from behind, causing that familiar tingling all over my body.

"I wanna tell you something." He started out.

Uh oh. I thought something bad was about to come out of his mouth.

"Yesterday I went to a bitch's I used to fuck with and spent some time with her. It was all business on my part, to get the information we needed to handle shit last night." He said backing up a step.

I turned around on the stool facing him, back straight up. Every part of me wanted to jump up off this chair and slap the hell out of him. But I held my control and calmed myself down.

"She gave you what you needed?" Sarcasm lacing my words.

"It wasn't like that. She had tried to take it there but it was only business for me. I wanted to tell you straight up, so there's nothing hanging over what we got. I wanna keep shit good, and build something solid. Lifetime shit."

"I'll give you one pass. See the thing is, it's not that you did what you did for business. I understand that. And I believe you when you say nothing happened, because right now I trust you. You've shown me the real ass man you are. But next time, I need you to come to me and tell me what's up first. You might be a stand up dude, but these hoes ain't shit. Especially with a fine ass paid man. I need to know what's going on!" I emphasized.

"I can do that. As long as we're good, I'm good." He came closer, kissing my forehead.

This was the growth I had made. No more fits and fights for no good reason. That side to me wouldn't come out unless it needed to. This was that grown ass woman shit to match the love I was getting from my man.

My phone buzzed in the pocket of my pajama joggers. I pulled it out and grumbled under my breath then hit the ignore button.

It was the same number that had been calling a few times this week. Dominque had left a message obviously drunk or high slurring about wanting to see BJ the other night. I knew I would have to pick up and answer one of these days. But not today. Today was all about love and my family. Today nobody was ruining that shit.

Nya

Pulling into the parking lot and seeing all the cars already parked, I knew some shit was up. I couldn't understand why we were headed here anyway. But figured we were just stopping by the strip club owned by Saint on our way to dinner or something. It was too early for this place to be turned the hell up like all the cars in the parking lot suggested. It was only around 10 o'clock.

It took me longer than I wanted to get ready tonight. Of course the dress fit perfectly and I paired it with some black red bottoms that I hadn't had a chance to wear yet. Saint surprised me with another gold and diamond chain that went with my other one.

He looked good as hell himself in his Gucci suit to match my black dress. We didn't even ride over in his car. When we came out of the front door of our house, he had a stretch limo waiting. This was some fairy tale shit. Even though Saint spoiled me, he had never done so much romantic shit. He would get me what I wanted but nothing over the top.

With all the shit going down and him being away, everything was a whirlwind. We hadn't had a chance to go on many dates or do some of the extravagant shit that I looked forward to in our future. Now that I had a damn future to look forward to.

After stepping out of the limo in front of Saint and him getting out standing up tall by my side, He lifted his arm for me to take. Walking in I felt like a celebrity. There was even a photographer right at the entrance. As soon as we stepped inside the door, the lights blinded me, not expecting the shit.

I gave Saint a look, "What did you do bae? You didn't have to do all this." I said honestly.

"I know I didn't have to do shit shawty. But for you, I'll do anything. So don't start that shit. Let me spoil my bitch. Tonight's all for you." He finished and leaned down placing a kiss on my lips parting them and showing me how much he meant what the hell he said.

Damn what did I do to deserve this nigga? He was perfect.

I didn't object and continued walking letting him lead me wherever he wanted. It was obvious he planned this shit. He went all the way to the front of the transformed room. As we walked further into the building I let my eyes roam around taking in the magnitude of decorations, people and the whole set up. Everything was out of this world beautiful. Decorated in Black and white with crystals everywhere. The shit looked like a completely different place. He really pulled this shit off.

A few niggas nodded their heads and spoke to Saint on the way to our table, but not one bitch spoke to me. That figured. Just like these tight ass bitches to be hating. But at least their asses knew not to try and talk to my man. I was content with knowing he was all mine. I would hate to have to fuck up all the shit Saint planned busting a bitch's face in. But I would do it in a heartbeat.

There was a table set for 6 right below the circular stage. Jolie and Drew were already seated as we joined them. The place was decorated like a wedding reception with fancy ass tables, centerpieces, and the crowd was more subdued than a typical club would be. There was some rap playing in the background, but not overbearing loud. So people couldn't talk to each other. All the guest were formally dressed. What the hell was Saint up to?

"Damn girl! That dress is fire." I told Jolie.

She was wearing a white mini dress that clung to her curves. Jolie was built and stacked in all the right places. I knew she was self-conscious but she honestly had no reason to be. I often wished I had an ass and titties like hers. Drew damn sure didn't mind. His hands were strategically placed on her thigh and one draped across her shoulders. Yeah, his ass was staking his claim.

"Bitch, you know we gotta shut shit down." She responded.

I was glad to see her upbeat attitude was back. This was Jolie.

"What are we drinking?"

"Let's do a bottle of Henny and take some shots. Saint you did the damn thing brother." Jolie complimented.

"I'm with it. Aye, But no showing out." Saint looked like a damn father between me and his sister.

Both of us smiled and gave his ass a look, like "yeah okay whatever nigga." He should know better. If we wanted to cut up, we would and he would be right here watching us.

But we would chill for a while and enjoy our dinner at least. Everything was catered and the food choices were some of the best shit I had ever eaten. The courses came and went, and our table seemed to be in a world of its own. The attention from being close to stage almost in front of all the other tables didn't even bother me. I was on cloud nine right now.

"So who are the other seats for?" I asked. I figured whoever else was coming would have been here by now since it was almost time for dessert.

"Don't worry 'bout that shit." Saint answered.

I shrugged and left it alone. I saw a giant cake rolled out to the center of the stage. It was at least five tiers and all white. There was writing on the side and top but couldn't make it out since it was in small letters.

I stood up along with the other guests when some cute older black woman came onto the microphone. The woman looked really familiar. I couldn't remember where I knew her from, but then when she started talking some more it hit me.

This was the same woman that had come to my rescue at the hotel after Saint was shot and I got raped. How the hell did Saint pull this off? It couldn't have been a coincidence.

I looked up and smiled wide, beaming at the man I loved. "How did you know?"

"I keep telling yo' ass I'm that nigga. I got you shawty."

Just then, he grabbed my hand and led me up to the stage. I was caught up talking to him and didn't catch what the sweet older lady said. Once we got closer, I came up to her and gave her a hug lingering for a moment. This woman was a true hero. Without her, I could've died on the street instead of making it to the hospital.

She pulled back and then held my other hand stepping to the side so I had a clear view of the top of the big ass cake in front of me now. The top read, the date and Congratulations. I was still confused until Saint let go of my other hand and dropped down to one knee.

Fuck. Was this really happening?

"NyAsia Miller you're all I ever want. The best thing that ever happened to me. You got my mothafuckin' heart shawty. Will you marry me?"

Of course he had to curse and the gangsta in him came through. This was the man I loved and I was just as hood as his ass. We were made for each other. I nodded my head as he stood up, pulling me into an embrace, lifting me off my feet. Everything seemed to disappear around us, until we kissed and the entire building erupted in a chorus of cheers, claps and yelling.

Who would have thought a bitch like me would have come straight from the bottom to the top after everything I had been through. God was real. This shit was almost too good to be true. Saint let me down and then I saw them.

Right at the bottom of the stage in front of us. A small group of people had pushed their way to the edge of where we were standing.

I looked down in disbelief, tears running down my face, then looked at Saint, "How?"

He looked confused as hell and turned back to look at the people in the front row a few feet away. Tears of happiness fell from my eyes. I had prayed and wished for this day to come. Saint really outdid himself. My thought to be dead parents stood in front of me, very much alive. I was in shock.

I leaned in giving the man I loved another deep kiss, savoring the feeling of what he had done for me. When we pulled back, screams rang out around us. I turned my head back to the crowd and that's when my heart broke.

Both of my parents were holding guns, drawn and aimed directly at me and Saint.

To be continued...

Hood Series

Hood Love and Loyalty 1
Hood Love and Loyalty 2
Hood Love and Loyalty 3

Gangsta Love Series

A Gangsta's Pledge
A Gangsta's Pledge 2
A Gangsta's Pledge 3
A Gangsta's Pledge 4 *(coming December 2018)*